MR. MARCH

HEROES OF ROGUE VALLEY: CALENDAR GUYS
BOOK 3

ANN ROTH

All rights reserved.

No part of this publication may be sold, copied, distributed, reproduced or transmitted in any form or by any means, mechanical or digital, including photocopying and recording or by any information storage and retrieval system without the prior written permission of both the publisher, Oliver Heber Books and the author, Ann Roth, except in the case of brief quotations embodied in critical articles and reviews.

PUBLISHER'S NOTE: This is a work of fiction. Names, characters, places, and incidents either are the product of the author's imagination or are used fictitiously. Any resemblance to actual persons, living or dead, business establishments, events, or locales is entirely coincidental.

Copyright © 2015 Ann Roth

Published by Oliver-Heber Books

0 9 8 7 6 5 4 3 2 1

 Created with Vellum

INTRODUCTION

Welcome to Ann Roth's exciting new series, Heroes of Rogue Valley: Calendar Guys series. Twelve months, 12 gorgeous firefighter heroes and the women who steal into their hearts and forever change their lives.

Meet Mr. March:

Firefighter Gus Viggio needs to convince the stubborn great aunt who raised him and recently suffered a stroke to give up the house that has become too much for her. When she refuses, Gus enlists help from her flamboyant hairstylist, Wanda Lippman. The two women get along well, and Gus's great aunt just might listen to Wanda. Wanda and Gus have both been hurt by love, and neither is ready to venture back into those dangerous waters anytime soon. But sometimes the heart knows best...

Mr. March—Gus Viggio
    Age 33, 6'4" tall, 230 pounds
    Single
    Proud Senior Firefighter
    Time with Guff's Lake Fire Department: 13 years

1

———

The second Gus Viggio offered his great aunt Polly a boost into his Jeep Cherokee, she shook her cane and fixed him with that stubborn *I'm not a helpless old lady yet* look that warned him to back off. God help him if he attempted to buckle her in.

Hands shoved into his jeans pockets, he stood by the open passenger door. Just in case. She wasn't as strong as she used to be, and those arthritic hands made even fastening the seatbelt difficult.

While he waited, he squinted against the sun, bright but not strong enough to take the chill out of the April morning. Almost overnight, spring had sprung in the Rogue Valley. Here in Guff's Lake, grass, shrubs and flowers, dormant through the winter, had made up for lost time and grown by leaps and bounds.

"My yard is mess," Aunt Polly lamented.

Once an avid gardener, she could no longer handle yard work. Gus had taken over the job, with occasional help from his father. "Dad and I will stop by and take care of it this weekend."

Maintaining the large front and back yards took a big chunk of time, but Gus didn't mind. He loved Aunt

Polly dearly. When his mom had left, his great aunt had invited him and his dad to move in and had raised Gus as her own.

Years ago, they'd decided to dispense with the "great" label, respectively shortening their names to "Aunt Polly" and "nephew." Not that "aunt" cut it, either. She was more a mother and grandmother rolled into one. He would do anything for her. Anything.

Buckled in at last, Aunt Polly folded her hands in her lap. "What are we waiting for?" she said with an impish look. "Let's boogie."

He grinned at her word choice. "You're in a good mood today."

"On such a beautiful morning, how could I not be?" She slipped a pair of sunglasses over her bifocals. "Besides, it isn't every day my favorite nephew and two of his fellow firefighters take me to lunch at Ellen's."

The stuffy restaurant wasn't at the top of Gus's go-to list, but his aunt loved eating there, and his buds enjoyed her company, so they tolerated the place.

"Your *only* nephew," he reminded her, pulling on his Ray-Bans.

"If I had a dozen, you'd still be my favorite."

"Not favorite enough to take my advice."

Her lips thinned. "Don't you dare start in on me about my living arrangements, Augusto Frances Viggio. I'm perfectly able to take care of myself, and you know it."

The use of Gus's full name meant she was seriously irritated, but didn't change the fact he disagreed with her.

Insisting on independence, she lived alone in her big, old house. No amount of reasoning or cajoling had convinced her to downsize and move into an apartment in a retirement community.

She did allow him to chauffeur her around, thanks to a stroke ten months ago that had put an end to her driving. Gus didn't mind shuttling her where she needed to go—when he could. Between him and his dad, they managed.

"If and when I decide to leave, I promise to let you know," she added. "But don't hold your breath." Raising her chin, she changed the subject. "As I was saying, you are my favorite nephew. Who else can I rely on to take me to my weekly hair appointment with Wanda?"

Gus tabled the conversation about moving—for the moment. "No problem."

Tommie's Hair and Nails was an easy ten-minute drive from Aunt Polly's house. "I need to schedule an inspection at Tommie's. May as well set that up today."

"For the safety project?"

"That's the one."

Gus had been tasked with checking fire and smoke alarms in every commercial and multi-dwelling residential structure as well as updating computer diagrams with the safest routes into and out of each. Important information that was posted in every building for both civilians and emergency responders to use during emergencies.

Gathering and collating all that data in the town of almost twenty-thousand people was taking more time than Gus had estimated. When he'd started ten weeks earlier, he'd promised the captain a finish date of early August. As tight as the deadline now seemed, he intended to deliver, even if it meant working off the clock.

No longer cross with him, Aunt Polly tilted her lips into a fond smile. "Not just anyone is strong and smart enough to be a firefighter. I'm so proud of you."

Gus's chest expanded. Not one for big displays of emotion, he gave a modest shrug.

"I can't wait to tell Wanda about lunch today," Aunt Polly said. "She'll be all ears. She's a darling, that one."

Darling wasn't the word that came to mind when Gus thought of Wanda Lipmann, who looked to be in her late twenties. He never knew what to expect when he saw her. Short and curvy, she wore her clothes bright and tight, and she changed her hair-style and color a couple times a month. Talk about unsettling.

They hadn't spoken much, except to say hi and bye when he brought Aunt Polly in and picked her up.

His aunt cast him a sly look. "If you'd get to know Wanda, you'd realize how special she is."

Gus narrowed his eyes. "Stop right there. You are not fixing me up—now or ever."

"But it's been almost a year since your breakup with Delores."

"Denise," he corrected. "I'm way over her."

For sure. After she'd pressured him one too many times to get married, he'd decided to break up with her. Then Aunt Polly had had her stroke. "Trust me, if I had time, I'd be dating. I happen to have a lot on my plate."

Between working at the Guff's Lake Fire Department, looking after Aunt Polly, and running his one-man classic car restoration business, Gus was overbooked.

Not that he wanted to give up any of his responsibilities. His car business relaxed him and felt more like play. Currently, he was restoring a 1965 classic Lincoln. His customer had agreed to pay top dollar, with a bonus if he finished in time for the classic car show in mid-May.

Whipping off her sunglasses, Aunt Polly gave him

the no-nonsense look that had always worked during her librarian days, her still-bright eyes serious behind the bifocals. "At thirty-two, you're not getting any younger."

"Don't hold back."

"Have I ever? It's time you found a wife and settled down. That should be your priority, but because it isn't, you need help. Mine."

She'd been after him to get married since the day he turned thirty, nagging him with a dogged determination that wouldn't quit.

Gus narrowed his eyes a fraction. "Stop."

"I will not." She sniffed. "Come October, I'll be eighty. I've earned the right to speak my mind."

"Like that's anything new. You know I'm not against marriage, but there's no guarantee it'll happen."

"Pish posh," Aunt Polly said. "Of course it will."

His parents had split up when he was seven, but he had good little-kid memories. Settling down and having two or three children appealed to him. But to date, every one of his serious relationships had gone south.

In matters of the heart, he'd begun to think he was just like his father. This apple hadn't fallen far from the tree.

Gus pulled onto Brewster Street, home to a dozen small businesses on the west side of town. Tommie's Hair and Nails salon was always buzzing, mostly with women, and judging by the number of cars parked in the salon lot, this morning was no different.

"This is a wash-and-trim appointment. I'll be done in about thirty minutes," his aunt said as opened the passenger door for her. "Since you need to schedule that inspection, you may as well wait inside."

Having just come off forty-eight hours—two back-to-back shifts—at the Guff's Lake Fire Department, with a couple calls in the dead of night, Gus planned to grab some quick Z's in the Jeep while Aunt Polly had her hair done. He'd deliver her to Wanda, schedule the inspection, then make a beeline for the Jeep.

Refusing his arm, she relied on her cane. In the sunlight, the sparkly Tommie's Hair and Nails sign on the door glittered. Gus ushered his aunt inside and removed his shades.

The half-dozen or so females in the process of manicures and haircuts stopped chattering and stared at him.

Every week he brought Aunt Polly here, but you'd think they'd never seen him in the salon. Maybe it was his size. Bigger than many men, he'd grown used to curious looks. Lately, more than usual, thanks to the firefighter calendar.

Feeling awkward, he nodded at Carol Sue, who had about ten years on him.

"Nice to see you, Polly. Hi there, Gus," she said, batting her lashes at him.

"Hey," he replied, courteous but not too friendly.

A flirt and a gossip, Carol Sue lived to spread rumors. Here in Guff's Lake, information spread faster than a forest fire in summer. Gus preferred to stay out of her stories.

"Who do I talk to about scheduling a salon inspection?" he asked.

"That would be either Tommie or Wanda. Tommie's out just now, but Wanda is here. I'll let her know you and Polly have arrived. Help yourselves to coffee. The one with the orange band is the decaf you want, Polly. The other is leaded. Enjoy." She sashayed off.

Gus got Aunt Polly settled on the sofa and brought her a decaf with sugar and creamer. He filled a Styrofoam cup with the leaded stuff and sat in a chair. A few sips in, the "Employees Only" door at the rear of the salon opened. Wanda and two stylists stepped inside.

Sticking close to the door, all three glanced his way and whispered. God knew what they were saying. As long as it didn't go on too long, Gus didn't care.

He took another few sips of coffee before Wanda started forward.

POLLY BECKER RANKED among Wanda's favorite customers. She wasn't so comfortable with Polly's great nephew.

At six foot four and two hundred thirty pounds—details everyone who owned a Guff's Lake Fire Department calendar knew—Gus, aka Mr. March, was a strikingly handsome man. All solid muscle, he was built more like a super-fit linebacker than a firefighter. The piercing green eyes and short, light-brown hair with a hint of red didn't hurt, either. Looking at him, a woman would have to be dead not to have heart palpitations.

The calendar, sold to raise money for the station's benefit fund, had turned Gus and the eleven men featured into local celebrities.

Nadia, a stylist and close friend Wanda had been chatting with in back, elbowed her. "He always drops Polly off and leaves," she said in a low voice. "Carol Sue says he wants to talk to you today. I wonder why?"

"What does it matter, as long as I'm in the same room as him?" murmured Rochelle, Wanda's second closest friend. She worked from noon to closing on Wednesdays, but had come in early to accommodate a customer. She fanned herself. "He's even more gorgeous in person."

In place of his usual T-shirt, jeans and weathered leather jacket, he'd switched it up in a pressed blue shirt, dark pants and polished black oxfords. He looked good in dress clothes, but he looked equally fine in casuals.

"Maybe I'll move my schedule around and start working early on Wednesdays." Rochelle gave Wanda a sideways glance. "Unless you have dibs on him?"

Currently, both Rochelle and Nadia were single and in the market for a boyfriend. Wanda frowned. "Tommie depends on you to work late Tuesdays and Wednesdays. And don't forget, I'm taking a break from men."

Her friends shared a look. "You say that every time you go through a breakup," Nadia pointed out. "Until some cute guy asks you out. Then you're off and running again."

"After I've turned down every guy who asked me out the past six-and-a-half months? If that isn't serious, I don't know what is."

She refused to date until she figured out how to win and hold a man's love with more than good sex. She had the sex part down but not the rest, and her heart had been broken more times than she could count.

The latest split with Larry had hurt almost as much as losing Wayne ten years earlier. In hindsight, she realized much of the pain stemmed from her seriously wounded pride. She'd tried her best to keep Larry interested but had failed. Yet again. She didn't think she could survive one more breakup.

"To clarify," Rochelle said, "you're not interested in Gus Viggio."

"Right."

Even if a mere glance at the man caused a spike in her pulse rate, he'd never given her more than a brief greeting and a cursory glance. A good thing, too. Otherwise, she might be tempted to forget she'd sworn off guys, proving her friends right.

"Polly's waiting for me," she said. "And apparently so is Gus."

Curious as she was about what he could possibly want, she paused and fluffed her layered, purple-streaked, blond hair—a far cry from its dull-brown natural color. She strutted forward, her teal, three-inch ankle boots clicking smartly across the tile floor. The walk had taken years to perfect.

As she drew closer, Gus pushed to his feet. His great aunt had raised him right.

"Morning, Polly," Wanda said, with a warm smile.

The older woman beamed. "I like your hair, Wanda. Those purple streaks are fun. And what a snazzy outfit."

"Thanks." Wanda smoothed her short-sleeve, lavender tee over her hips. Even with the three extra inches of the ankle boots, she was only five feet six. She tilted her head back a little to greet the firefighter. "Hello, Gus."

He nodded, his expression impossible to read, and gave her a once-over from her head to the hint of cleavage, courtesy of the low scoop neck, where his gaze lingered a beat longer than an uninterested man's should have. Then past her flared, teal skirt to her black leggings.

Pride surged through her. As with her walk, the cutting-edge hairstyles and clothing had never been natural to her. Neither was being bubbly and talkative. But wanting to be noticed and liked by men, even though she'd temporarily sworn off them, she'd adjusted. Her efforts had paid off. Getting a date when she wanted one was never a problem, and both male and female customers kept coming back.

Proving Cindy right, for once.

"I'm told you're the one to see about scheduling a safety inspection," he said, his deep, sexy voice vibrating through her.

Safety inspection—of course. A little part of her had assumed he wanted information of the personal kind. What a relief he didn't. Or so she assured herself. Yet something inside her deflated a fraction. "I'm the one, all right."

"Do you have any time Monday?"

"We're closed that day, but I guess that'd work."

"If you're closed, who'll let me in?"

"Either Tommie or me."

Likely Wanda. Tommie had just turned sixty-five and decided to retire at the end of September. Wanda wanted to buy the business and the building—provided she saved up enough for the down-payment necessary to secure a loan. Although she still needed a fair chunk of change, she'd assured Tommie that when the time came, she would have the required funds.

The past few months, Tommie had been teaching her the ins and outs of running the salon, and slowly giving Wanda more responsibility.

"Your aunt should be ready to go in about a half hour," she told Gus. "You can pick her up then."

"He's going to wait here today." Polly showered him with a fond grin. "Then he's taking me to lunch at Ellen's."

No wonder he'd dressed up. "Lucky you." Wanda sighed.

She'd always wanted to try the upscale restaurant, but not one of her boyfriends had ever taken her there. "Have a seat in the waiting area, Gus. I'll bring her to you when we finish. Come on, Polly, let's make you gorgeous."

She offered her arm, but Polly rebuffed her. Thanks to her shoes, Wanda stood some two inches over the woman. She also moved a lot quicker. She slowed way down, and they made their way to her station across the way.

Or tried.

Polly dug in her heels and waved her cane at Gus. "Aren't you coming with us?"

"My station is small, and there's no place for you to sit," Wanda pointed out. "You'll be more comfortable in the waiting area."

So would she. If he hovered around, she wouldn't be able to relax.

"Nonsense. He'll bring a seat with him," Polly insisted. "I want him to see what you do."

"Aunt Polly..."

Wanda didn't understand Gus's warning look."

Lips compressed, Polly turned away from his gaze.

While he returned to the waiting area to grab a chair, Wanda helped her into the salon chair. She fastened a large plastic smock around Polly's neck, gently tipped her back to wash her hair, and wondered what her customer was up to.

2

———

Muttering, Gus carried a café chair that was too small for him from the waiting area to Wanda's station. Not long after he sat down, the women in the salon quit with the wondering looks and returned to chatting, laughing and whatever else they did. Dozing in the car would have suited him better, but he didn't want his great aunt talking him up with her hairstylist.

Wanda sure knew her way around a pair of scissors, shaping Aunt Polly's hair while keeping up a lively conversation. His great aunt seemed engrossed in her every word, and often offered her own comments. Wanda was also funny. More than once, Gus cracked up. A couple times, Aunt Polly even laughed.

He couldn't get over that. Since the stroke, she rarely laughed, not full-out like this. How did Wanda do that?

She was too flamboyant for his tastes. Put off by her wild clothes and hair, he'd never really noticed her beyond the usual once-over all red-blooded guys gave women.

But she changed her look so often he didn't know who she was. Maybe that was her point, to keep him and everyone else from figuring her out. It bothered him.

She did have big, expressive eyes and a great mouth, although he didn't care for the blue lipstick. Sweet curves, too—large breasts, a small waist, and rounded hips. She bent forward to whisper something in Aunt Polly's ear, her flouncy skirt rising just enough to offer a tantalizing glimpse of the backs of her leggings-covered thighs.

He couldn't see any higher, but his healthy male imagination filled in the blanks.

"...Still not dating, dear?" Aunt Polly said. In the mirror, she met his gaze as in, pay attention, Gus.

He rolled his eyes, but she'd already glanced away.

"Not yet." Wanda shook her head. "I need the break."

"Larry wasn't good enough for you."

Wanda's lush lips pursed, and Gus got so lost in watching her mouth move he didn't pay much attention to her reply.

"I wish you'd been there to tell him so," she finished.

"I would have, too." Aunt Polly nodded toward Gus. "You're not the only one with romance troubles. Delores, Gus's last girlfriend, wasn't—"

"Denise," he corrected. "And leave me out of this."

"Don't be a grump, Gus. I guess we should have left you in the waiting area, after all."

Let her feed some bull story about his love life to Wanda? No way.

Wanda caught his attention in the mirror and lifted an eyebrow—only one. How did she do that?

Her eyes twinkled. "You look as if you just ate a brussels sprout."

"How did you know about me and brussels sprouts?" he asked.

"I don't like them, either. Maybe if they're smothered in chocolate..."

She made an awful face, and they both laughed. One glance at Aunt Polly's smug I knew you'd like each other expression, and Gus sobered right up.

Oblivious, Wanda ran a comb through his aunt's hair, then spritzed her head with a fruity-smelling mist. "There," she said. "You're all done."

His aunt cast a critical look at her reflection. Wanda gave her a hand mirror and turned the chair so she could check out the back.

"Not much I can do about all these wrinkles and sagging jowls, but you always make me feel pretty, Wanda. I'll bet I could pass for seventy-two or three. What do you think, Gus?"

He and Wanda shared another smile. "You definitely could, Aunt Polly. You did a great job, Wanda."

"Thank you both, but when I work on someone who could be a super model, it's easy. Wrinkles and jowls, my foot."

Wanda curtsied, coaxing another chuckle out of him. Like his aunt, he hadn't laughed this much in ages.

"I believe I'll go powder my nose," Aunt Polly said.

Wanda helped her from the chair and handed her the cane. "You want me to go with you?"

"I don't need any help. You and Gus wait for me at the front desk."

Chin up, she toddled forward about as fast as a turtle crossing the street.

"Your aunt is a very special lady," Wanda said, pulling a broom from the corner to sweep the silvery hair that had fallen on the floor. "You're lucky to have her."

"Don't I know it. Although there are times when she drives me crazy."

"I can see how she would. I worry about her, living alone."

"So do my dad and I, but she refuses to move into a retirement community."

"She wants to be independent."

"She's also as stubborn as they come."

"I've noticed." Wearing a pensive expression, Wanda put the broom away. "There's something different about her today, a lovely gleam in her eyes I haven't seen since before the stroke. Isn't it wonderful that she keeps improving!"

"I wish, but she isn't getting any better. The thing is..." Gus hesitated, but Wanda needed to know. "She thinks you and I should go on a date."

"Us?" Wanda looked as bewildered as he felt. "You're kidding."

"Nope. She wants more than that—to see me married and settled."

"With me?" Wanda threw back her head and laughed.

He was used to women coming on to him, and found her reaction off-putting. Even if he wasn't interested in her. "It's not that funny," he said. "She's serious. I haven't dated in a while. I'm not into it right now. She thinks I need a push."

"I guess Denise did break your heart."

"Nah. I don't know where my aunt got that idea. She seems to think Larry did a number on you."

"He did."

He waited for her to elaborate, but she was busy shaking out the bib Aunt Polly had worn.

"Love hurts," he said.

"A lot. So Polly wants you to find your Ms. Right, but you're not interested."

"I wouldn't mind settling down with someone. But finding her is no picnic." He shook his head. "Sometimes I wonder if I ever will."

Her big eyes flashed empathy. "I know exactly what you mean."

Thanks to Larry, he meant to say, but something different came out of his mouth. "I've never seen eyes that color."

"I'm wearing violet contact lenses. My eyes are actually on the brown side of hazel."

"Nearsighted?"

She shook her head. "Perfect vision. Changing my hair, clothes and eye color keeps things interesting."

And also kept others at a distance, but that was no concern of his.

She fluttered her lashes in a blatant flirtation he enjoyed despite himself. Yet she laughed at the idea of dating him. The mixed signals confused him. "You're an unusual woman."

"I'll take that as a compliment."

She flashed a bright smile that didn't quite ring true, and wasn't half as pretty as the real thing.

"You sure are great with Aunt Polly," he said, wanting to see it again.

That worked. Her whole face lit up. Much better.

"That's easy. I enjoy her company."

Captivated, he held her gaze. "She feels the same about you."

Something hot and seductive passed between them that just about knocked him off his feet.

Wanda jerked her gaze away. "Your aunt is probably on her way to the front desk."

Gus cleared his throat. "Don't want to keep her waiting. Let's go."

~

AT THE FRONT DESK, Wanda didn't so much as glance Gus's way. She couldn't. Standing together in her station, she swore they'd shared a moment. The electrifying kind that sparked through her and made her want things she had no business wanting, not until she figured out how to win and hold a man's love. She needed to learn how to read a man better, so that once the thrill of new-partner sex wore off, the relationship continued.

After paying for the trim, Polly handed her a tip. "For you."

"Aw, thanks, Polly." Wanda stuck the money in her skirt pocket. Tips and whatever else she managed to put aside went into the savings account earmarked for the down payment on the salon.

"Why don't you have lunch with us today?" Polly asked.

Wanda's gaze skittered toward Gus. Not quite meeting her eyes, he pulled on the open collar of his shirt, as it were too tight.

Message received. He didn't want her there.

Wanda didn't blame him. He probably wanted to enjoy lunch alone with his aunt. Besides, they hardly knew each other. Certainly not well enough to share a meal orchestrated by Polly.

Gus was no more interested in her than she was in him. In other words, not at all. That moment she'd thought they'd shared? A figment of her imagination.

"I can't," she said. "I'm booked solid for the rest of

the day, and I'll barely have time for a break." Which was God's honest truth.

His unmistakable relief stung a little but further underlined her resolve. There would be no getting involved with a man until she solved the twin puzzles of what he wanted, and how to hold his interest.

Wanda knew what Gus didn't want—her. This was good, and effectively eliminated any wondering how to hold his interest. Her brief foray into the land of warmth and hope that this time would be different had been a silly lapse. She pushed it from her mind, then mentally brushed her hands together.

From this moment on, she would think of Gus as Polly's nephew, period.

3

Living forty-eight hours straight every week with eleven crewmates and the captain, Gus knew more about each of them than he did his own mother. A lot more, as he and his mom had never been close. These guys were family for life, brothers he trusted completely.

Aunt Polly doted on each crewmember, and the feelings were mutual. Before the stroke, she'd made a habit of stopping by the station with cookies and breads. Now that she didn't bake anymore, she'd taken to inviting a couple guys at a time to lunch with her and Gus. She offered to pay, but they usually went dutch treat.

Like Gus, Owen and Max had traded their jeans, tees and sneakers for dress clothes. They would have preferred lunch at Rosemary's or The Rogue, two more casual places to eat, but Aunt Polly had insisted on Ellen's.

Seated at a cloth-covered table in a room filled mainly with well-dressed women picking at salads and sandwiches, Gus, Owen and Max finished with pie and coffee, their big hands dwarfing the dainty cups.

Sticking with decaf, Aunt Polly took a few bites of her pie before she patted her 'do. "Lunch is almost over, and no one has said anything about my hair."

"I told you earlier that I like it," Gus said.

Despite being a computer geek, his best bud, Owen, knew how to make women feel special. He gave an approving smile. "Very nice. You're always beautiful, Polly."

She basked in the praise.

"I agree. You look good," Max, the best card player at the station, commented. "You're still a pretty lady."

"Oh, you boys. If only I was fifty years younger..."

Max grinned. "All the single guys at the department would be after you."

Aunt Polly tilted her head and lowered her eyelids a fraction. A widow for forty years, she still enjoyed flirting.

"Wanda at Tommie's Hair and Nails is a genius at hair, and a real doll. Just ask Gus."

Everyone knew his aunt wanted him to settle down, and he gave a What can you do? shrug. By Owen and Max's interested expressions, they wanted to hear more about the hairstylist his aunt considered a good choice for him.

Gus couldn't believe she'd asked Wanda to lunch. Lunches with the crew were sacred to her. Until today, she'd never invited anyone else along.

He pictured the meal, Wanda sitting between him and Aunt Polly, and Owen and Max pulling out all stops to impress her. She'd soak up the attention, flirt and make them laugh as she had Gus, drawing them in with her big eyes and hypnotic, kiss-me mouth. About now one of them would be asking her out. Gus had no idea whether she'd take up the offer of whoever asked, but the whole idea ticked him off.

Good thing she had appointments all day.

Owen, Max and Aunt Polly were staring at him, waiting for his reply. "Wanda's okay," he said. "I need more coffee." He signaled the waitress for a refill.

"What do you three have planned for the rest of the day?" Aunt Polly asked while a young, pretty server refilled their cups. Her friendly manner and welcoming smile signaled interest, but Gus wasn't about to strike up a conversation, and neither were his buds. Not with Aunt Polly at the table.

"Grab a nap," Max replied, his eyes weary.

"Same here." Owen yawned. "We had a rough night."

"Two fires and three medical emergencies, Gus told me. Are either of you on medical duty this month?"

The Guff's Lake Fire Department required firefighters to be certified paramedics. Crewmembers rotated between firefighting and paramedic duties. This month, Gus was assigned to firefighter duty.

"Max and I are," Owen said. "That middle call last night..." Grimacing, he scrubbed the back of his neck.

"Oh, dear." Aunt Polly tsked in sympathy. "Did you lose a patient?"

"Almost. Thanks to the quick actions of the night nurse at the retirement community where the woman lives, we got her stabilized and into the ER in time."

It was common knowledge Gus wanted his aunt to move to a place like that. Silently thanking Owen for the plug, he nodded. "The staff at those places is well-trained to handle emergencies."

Aunt Polly's mouth tightened. "I am not moving to a retirement home."

There was no convincing the impossible woman.

Stifling a few choice words, Gus put up his hands. "Okay."

For a few moments, she glared at him. Then the conversation jumped to the great weather they'd been having, and the next few minutes passed smoothly.

Tired of treading carefully and meaningless chitchat, Gus drained the last of his coffee. "Ready to go?"

"Let me powder my nose."

Refusing offers of help, Aunt Polly excused herself and made her way toward the restrooms.

The fussy lunch over, Gus blew out a breath and signaled for the check.

"What was all that about your aunt's hairdresser?" Owen asked while they waited for Aunt Polly to return.

Gus snorted. "She's gotten it into her head that Wanda is the right woman for me."

"Is she?"

"Hell, no." They were as different as a house fire and a swim in Guff's Lake.

"What does she look like?" Owen said.

"She's about yea high." Gus tapped his hand against his pecs and searched for the right words to describe the bright clothes, crazy hair and colored contact lenses she didn't need. "She looks like a walk on the wild side," he summarized.

Owen and Max made approving guy sounds.

"She sounds hot," Max said.

Gus couldn't argue with that.

"What's stopping you from asking her out?"

"I'm not sure I want to. In the last year, we both went through bad relationships. I prefer a more natural woman."

"What do you mean?" Max asked.

"Not so much makeup and stuff."

Both of Gus's friends frowned.

"Someone who isn't afraid to be who she is," he added, thinking of his mom. At one time, she'd hidden her true self under clothes and makeup. She'd ended up hurting his dad—and him—real bad.

There was no room in his life for a woman like that.

Owen looked like he wanted to ask more questions. Not wanting to get into the ins and outs of the past he'd put behind him long ago, Gus moved on. "Neither of you has seen Aunt Polly in a while. How does she seem to you?"

Looking pensive, Max stroked his chin. "A little frail, but pretty good for a woman her age."

"You saw how hard it was for her to get up by herself, and look how long she's been in the bathroom."

Max frowned. "Think she's okay in there?"

"If she doesn't come out in a few minutes, I'll get someone to check on her. She'll give me hell for worrying. I wish she'd accept help from me or somebody. She's slipping." Going downhill and it scared him.

"She's seventy-nine and she had a stroke, remember?" Owen said. "Maybe she isn't as physically strong as she used to be, but her mind is razor sharp."

"Most of the time," Gus said. "Although the other day, she forgot my phone number."

"Hey, *I* forget your number. With a smart phone, who needs to remember details like that?" Owen squinted at him. "You're worried about her."

"Damn straight. Why do you think I keep harping on her to move out of that big old house and into an apartment at a retirement community? You saw her reaction to that."

"She's a stubborn old bird, all right," Max agreed. "How about a live-in?"

Gus had suggested full-time, at-home help, but Aunt Polly had panned that idea as well. Having a full-time nurse after the stroke had driven her mad. "She doesn't want anyone breathing down her neck. I don't think she has the funds for that, either. And she won't take money from me or my dad."

"Then how can she afford a place in a retirement community?" Owen asked.

"She owns the house free and clear. It needs work but has good bones and is in a nice neighborhood. She'd get a decent price for it that would more than cover the costs of an apartment. There are two or three retirement communities in town with good reputations that aren't too expensive. But she won't even consider looking, and if I bring it up, she gives me hell."

"My mom always listens to her sister," Owen said. "Is there someone in the family or a friend who could talk to her?"

"Aunt Polly's only sister passed away five years ago." Gus and their dad were the last blood relatives left.

"What about one of Polly's friends?"

"Her two closest friends are gone, but if they were still alive, I doubt she'd talk to them, let alone listen to their advice. She doesn't like to show her weaknesses to anyone—not even me or my dad."

Gus thought about Wanda and how Aunt Polly had sung her praises all day. If Wanda suggested the move, his great aunt might be more open.

While he and his crewmates continued to wait, they discussed baseball and upcoming draft picks. All the while, the idea of enlisting Wanda's help began to take root in Gus's mind.

When Aunt Polly finally rejoined them, she seemed exhausted. After hugging Max and Owen good-bye, she even let Gus take her arm.

On the drive home, she said little.

Worried, Gus glanced at her. "You okay?"

"I had a wonderful time, but like you, Max and Owen, I need a nap."

He pulled up the drive to the rambling house that tethered her in its invisible grasp. Moments later, he escorted her through the front door. Familiar sights and smells greeted him—the leaded glass windows in the entry, the oriental rug over the oak living room floor, the faint scent of his aunt's rose perfume.

She wasn't the only one who loved the place. Having grown up here, nurtured by her, Gus carried his own warm memories. But Aunt Polly could no longer handle the responsibility of home ownership.

By the time he got her comfortable in the Barcalounger where she liked to nap and kissed her weathered cheek good-bye, he'd made up his mind. He would definitely ask Wanda to talk to his aunt.

4

"You're frowning," Nadia observed as Wanda slid her cell phone into her pocket. Thursdays and Fridays they both worked the late shift. "Appointment cancellation or a call from home?"

Home was Tillamook, Oregon, where Wanda's mom and sister still lived. Cindy, who bristled at being called "Mom" because she didn't want people to guess her age, jumped from disaster to disaster, most of it her own making, and a phone call almost always signaled the latest Something Bad.

When things were going well, which they were at the moment, Wanda rarely heard from her. She shook her head. "I haven't heard from Cindy in weeks." She needed to call home and touch base. "But I did hear from my sister, Crystal. She's dating a guy who owns a lumber company, and Cindy is all agog at the possibilities of her first-born marrying into money. No, I was talking to Gus."

"Mr. March Gus? With his military-short hair, I'd bet my left hand he didn't call to schedule a trim." Nadia gave a sly grin.

"FYI, he isn't interested in me."

"Oh, no? I saw how he checked you out."

"It was the hair and outfit. And hey, he's a man. They're programmed to look at all women."

"Trust me, this particular male is definitely interested in you."

Nadia was mistaken. "I know when a guy is into me, and Gus isn't. It doesn't matter anyway, because I'm sticking to my plan."

Even if the mere thought of Gus Viggio made her go weak in the knees. No, it didn't. She squared her shoulders. "He called about Polly."

Nadia's knowing look turned into concern. "Oh, dear. She seemed her usual self when she was here yesterday."

"According to Gus, she's fine. He'll explain when we get together."

"I'm glad she's okay. This so-called meeting sounds mysterious...and romantic. When does it happen?"

"Tomorrow, before work. We're going to talk, period."

"A breakfast date can be very romantic."

"It isn't a date!"

Wanda's voice had risen. Across the way, Carol Sue and her customer, Betty Randall, a grandmotherly woman every bit as quick to spread the latest tidbit, stopped gossiping to stare.

Wanda elbowed Nadia, and they both lowered their voices.

"Where is he taking you?" Nadia asked.

"I'm driving myself. We're meeting at the Coffee Shack."

"Sounds like a first date to me."

Wanda gave her a dirty look. "Will you stop?"

"Have it your way. I can't wait to find out what this is about."

"You and me both."

THANKS TO A LAST-MINUTE call from Tommie, asking Wanda to stop at the salon and open up Thursday morning, she left late for the Coffee Shack. Too late to grab a desperately-needed first cup of coffee on the thirty-minute drive. If she wanted to arrive within five to ten minutes of the agreed-upon meeting time, she'd best hurry.

On her favorite oldies station, "Take It Easy" started to play. "Not this morning," she muttered.

After checking for traffic, she turned onto Kirkdale Road, the only road in town that ran straight from the north end of town to the south.

Gus would pick a meeting place way out by the actual Guff's Lake, the town's namesake on the edge of the city limits. Nestled in the foothills of the Siskiyou Mountains, the spectacular natural lake and nearby woods drew tourists and locals alike for hiking and fishing, with a large resort area to boot. In addition to the Guff's Lake Resort Hotel, with its spa, pool and tennis courts, there were shops and restaurants, vacation cabins, and boating on the four-mile-diameter lake.

None of which had anything to do with today's meeting.

What was so important that they had to meet miles away from Tommie's, and in person?

Dying to know, Wanda sped forward. Not too fast —she didn't need a ticket—but fast enough. She'd missed the morning rush, although pre-tourist season, traffic was rarely heavy.

On this bright, sunny morning, she cracked open both the sedan's front windows. Not enough to muss her hair, but enough to usher in the lovely scents of spring.

This was probably a good time to phone Cindy. Her mom worked swing shift at the Tillamook Ice Cream factory, but she'd be up by now. Wanda connected using her Bluetooth.

"Hey, baby," Cindy said, yawning. "It's been awhile. You must be calling with an update. What's his name?"

Briefly, Wanda thought of Gus. Why mention him, when there was nothing to tell? No sense getting Cindy all excited.

"I'm still single," she said.

"Why can't you be more like your sister? She never has any trouble getting a boyfriend."

After all these years, Wanda should have been used to the comparisons with her older sister that always found her lacking. But they still stung.

For as long as she could remember, Cindy had harped on her. She was too plain, too serious, too boring to ever attract a man, let alone hold onto him.

Wanda had taken the words to heart. By the time she entered high school, she'd turned herself into a talkative, vivacious teenager who wore attention-grabbing clothes that made boys sit up and take notice.

The new persona brought her popularity and attention and got Cindy off her case—for a while. Until the breakup with Wayne. It had been close to nine years, but her mother couldn't seem to move past the relationship that had ended when Wanda was twenty. Which was the reason she'd moved to Guff's Lake.

Refusing to get sucked into Cindy's negativity, Wanda drew in a calming breath. "I don't have any trouble getting a date, either. I happen to be taking a break from men."

"You're what?"

"Taking a break. I haven't had a date in months."

"And you're just now telling me? I'm only your mother." Cindy sounded hurt.

She also liked to dish out advice Wanda didn't need or want.

"You're twenty-eight, and you still don't have a husband," her mother pointed out. "You can't afford to take a break."

"I guess I'll have to risk it," Wanda replied through clenched jaws. "Tell me about Crystal. Is she happy?"

"Why wouldn't she be? Derrick is handsome and successful. In a way, he reminds me of Wayne."

Here we go. As Cindy began to glorify the "good old days," Wanda stifled a groan, tuned her out, and strolled down her own memory lane.

On the day varsity quarterback Wayne Doherty had asked Wanda out, her life had taken a one-eighty. Suddenly, she had more friends than she'd ever dreamed of. Following Cindy's advice, she was bubbly, funny and energetic at all times—even when she didn't want to be.

She focused on Wayne's happiness, doing what he wanted to do and letting him choose which movies and concerts to attend. Making his preferences hers, even when they weren't.

This had worked out so well that Wayne began to talk about getting married after he graduated to the pros. With the dream of becoming Mrs. Wayne Doherty, Wanda had followed him to the college that had offered him a football scholarship. She wasn't enrolled, but as lovers and best friends, they couldn't bear to be separated.

Less than a year later, everything fell apart. Wayne

met someone else. When he started his pro football career he took his new girlfriend along and left Wanda and their so-called love and friendship behind. A short time later, an injury put an end to his career. He married the girl anyway and now worked in her family's insurance business.

Since then, Wanda had been involved in a number of relationships. She hadn't been able to hold any man for long, including Larry.

Cindy was still blabbering away. Feeling inadequate and fed up, Wanda broke in. "Sorry. I have go."

She disconnected a mile or so before she reached the Coffee Shack.

Knowing Gus had zero romantic interest in her freed her from pretending. She wouldn't have to flirt, hang on to his every word or fake fascination when he bored her.

For the next little while she could let down and be herself.

If she could just remember how.

About a hundred feet ahead, a rabbit darted across the road. The CRV in front of Wanda swerved to avoid hitting the animal and crashed into the four-door going the opposite direction. The drivers exited their vehicles—thankfully, neither appeared hurt—and began talking, gesturing and pulling out their cell phones. They also blocked both directions of the two-lane road.

With no room to pull around, traffic ground to a halt. By the time the drivers pushed their cars into the meadow off the road and traffic resumed, fifteen minutes had passed.

Wanda glanced at her watch and groaned. Almost thirty minutes late. Gus no doubt assumed she'd stood him up. She thought about calling him, but with arrival time in about sixty seconds, she saw no point.

Whether he would still be waiting was anyone's guess.

5

<hr>

Gus rarely set foot in the Coffee Shack, mainly because it was twenty-plus miles from his place. He preferred Rosemary's Breakfast Nook, a five-minute drive from home and a few short blocks from the station. With its great food and convenient location, Rosemary's served as the go-to coffee, pastry and breakfast haunt for everyone at the fire department.

But crewmates and other fire department employees shuffled in and out of Rosemary's all the time, and people liked to talk. Explaining that his meeting with Wanda was strictly about Aunt Polly wouldn't keep them from speculating. Gus wanted to avoid that. Here on the outskirts of town, chances of running into anyone he knew were less likely.

Although tourist season was still weeks away, the café was packed. The spectacular view of Guff's Lake and the Siskiyou Mountains drew locals, especially on a clear day.

No sign of Wanda, but he'd arrived early. All his life, punctuality had been drilled into him, first by his father, then by the upper ranks at the fire department. As he'd anticipated, he didn't see a single familiar face, although people checked him out as they had at Tommie's yesterday.

When a couple in the corner got up to leave, Gus snagged the table for him and Wanda. Two women at the adjacent table gave him the eye. The brunette was attractive, but his attention stayed on the door.

After waiting fifteen minutes past the time they'd agreed on, he bought himself a coffee and a copy of the *Guff's Lake News*. He subscribed but had only read today's local sports section. By the time he finished the rest of the paper, another fifteen minutes had elapsed. Looked as if she wouldn't make it. He was reaching for his cell phone to reschedule when she walked in.

In a flouncy yellow dress that molded to her breasts and flared slightly at the hips, and red ankle boots, she was hard to miss. And damned sexy. As she swished into the room, everyone checked her out—especially the men.

She cast the flirty smile Gus recognized at several men. A guy in a flannel shirt and one dressed like a hotshot businessman both flashed return grins, the kind that meant they intended to hit on her. Seriously irritated, Gus caught their attention and narrowed his eyes in silent warning. The grins vanished, and both men diverted their attention elsewhere.

Wanda had spotted him. Gus forgot this was a meeting about his aunt and that Wanda wasn't his type. Eager for the heady impact of that flirtatious smile directed at him, he grinned, exactly like the bozos he'd just threatened.

Instead of showering him with that sassy smile, her expression cooled, her purple lips barely curving and the sway of her hips less exaggerated. Yesterday, he could have sworn she was interested in him. Confused, he stood.

"Sorry I'm so late," she said, breathless. "I'll explain after I get my coffee. I'm in desperate need of caffeine."

Ready for a refill himself, Gus grabbed his mug and accompanied her to the counter.

The kid taking orders looked like he should be in high school—way too young for Wanda. She didn't pay him much attention, but the guy did everything but drool over her. Gus gave him the same intimidating frown he'd used moments ago, with the same results. The kid straightened up.

"You're not wearing colored contacts today," Gus noted, squinting at her. "There's something else different about your eyes."

"I didn't have time to put on my full face this morning. I know I look awful. I'll fix it later."

"Not awful...different."

"I feel naked."

A loaded word, for sure. His imagination jumped to life, and a certain part of his body got real interested.

"What can I get you?" the kid asked.

"A jumbo-size, double-shot cappuccino." She studied the baked goods behind the glass counter. "Ooh, and look. You carry Samantha's scones. I've been seeing her treats in more and more places. Could I have a blueberry scone, warmed?"

"Make that two," Gus said. "And a refill on black coffee. I know Sam," he commented while they waited. "She and Adam, one of my crewmates, are hot and heavy. She's got a kid he's crazy about, too."

"Adam is a lucky man."

Gus agreed. After the short exchange, Wanda fell silent. She seemed different than usual, quieter and less animated. She must really need caffeine.

"Everything okay?" he asked.

"I'm dying for coffee, I could have used an extra half hour of sleep, and I skimped on my makeup," she said, her purple-painted lips hinting at a humorous smile. "Other than that, I'm fantastic."

This was more like it. Gus chuckled. After she drank some of her coffee, her sense of humor would likely return to full-strength.

When the kid set their order on the counter, Gus pulled out his wallet. "How much do I owe you?"

The boy opened his mouth, but Wanda spoke first. "We should pay separately."

"Hey, you drove all the way out here at my invitation," Gus said. "This is on me."

"As long as we're not on a date."

"Nope." He paid.

"Just making sure."

On the way to the table, he eyed her. "You made it clear you don't want to date me."

"Or anyone else."

"Okay."

"What do you care, Gus? You're not interested in me."

Wrong. He was definitely interested. Didn't mean he wanted to take her out.

She set her scone and coffee on the table, sat down and tasted the coffee. "Oh, that's good."

A perfect, purple imprint of her lips rimmed the edge of her mug. Lucky mug.

"Cappuccino foam...right here." He pointed out the place on his own mouth.

She licked the bubbles with the tip of her tongue. Gus didn't think she meant to be provocative, but sweet jeezus, she was. He couldn't tear his gaze from her lips.

She frowned. "Did I miss the spot?"

"Nope. You got it all." He downed more coffee, then started on his scone. "You were going to explain why you were late," he reminded her.

"Right. It all started at the ungodly hour of seven-thirty this morning, when Tommie woke me with a phone call. She asked me to open the salon. I'm the only employee with a door key and the password for the cash register."

She paused for more coffee and a bite of scone. "I couldn't unlock the doors and just leave. Our manicurist had scheduled an eight-thirty appointment and I assumed she'd arrive by eight-twenty. Instead she showed up at eight thirty-five because her customer had switched the appointment to eight forty-five.

"But I could have made it almost on time, if there hadn't been an accident a few miles from here. I should have phoned you, but I kept expecting the traffic to clear up."

"No big. You have a key to unlock the salon and you know the password to the cash register. You also scheduled the inspection. Are you managing the salon?"

Wanda shook her head. "Tommie's retiring at the end of September, and she's training me for when I buy the salon and the building."

Flirtatious, flamboyant Wanda, owning and running the salon? Gus was surprised. "That's a big job."

"One I'm ready for. I've been at Tommie's since I first moved to Guff's Lake seven years ago. I've worked as a receptionist and every other position except nails, and I know the salon inside and out. I also have an associate's degree in business. Someday—" She looked away. "Never mind. You didn't set up this meeting to listen to my big dreams."

Gus wanted to know. "I'd like to hear about them."

"All right, but don't laugh."

"I won't, unless you crack a joke."

"This is serious," she said, looking solemn. "I'm going to keep the services we have and add a day spa, similar to the one at Guff's Lake Resort."

Gus had never figured Wanda as ambitious. But then, aside from her frequent hair and eye-color changes, what did he really know about her?

"I have experience running a business," he said. "I own a small one. Very small. I'm the sole employee."

"What do you do?"

"Restore classic cars."

Her face lit up, and he figured the caffeine had hit. At last.

"I had no idea," she said. "I love classic cars."

"You do?"

She nodded. "Years ago, Cindy—my mom—married a man who owned a 1968 Mustang GT Coupe. That car was a total junker, but Brett had big plans to fix it up. I was only ten, but he let me hand him the tools he needed and he explained what he was doing. He promised me a ride in the finished car, only he and Cindy divorced before he got anywhere near that."

Cindy sounded almost as flaky as Gus's mom. "Last year, I restored that same make and model for a customer. Fully reconditioned, those babies can sell for forty or fifty thousand dollars."

"Wow. I never realized."

"It's true. So your parents are divorced."

"When I was four months old. That was Cindy's second divorce. My older sister, Crystal, has a different dad. He stuck around until she was three. Cindy married Brett when I was nine, and they divorced before I turned eleven."

"You and your sister were so young when your fathers left. I was seven when my parents split up."

"That's young, too, and probably tougher on you. I was too little to feel hurt, but I'll bet you did."

Gus nodded. "That and guilt-ridden. Before the split, my mom was always on my case, and I was sure her moving out was my fault."

"She left? That must have been awful. You know it wasn't your fault."

"As an adult I do, but until I was old enough to understand, I blamed myself."

Gus rarely talked about this. Why now, and why with Wanda?

She nibbled her scone and he got lost, watching her chew.

Puckers formed on her smooth brow. She wiped her lips with her napkin. "Is that better?"

His turn to frown. "Huh?"

"You were staring at my mouth."

"Was I? You're not funny today. The other day you were."

"Oh. I thought..." She switched before his eyes, fluttering her lashes and beaming a fakey smile his way. "Better?"

Much worse. He shook his head. "Go back to being yourself. We were talking about parents."

Her relieved expression puzzled him, but then everything about her today did. As much as he liked women, they often confused him.

"Is your mother Irish?" she asked. "Viggio is Italian, but with your green eyes and hints of red in your hair, you could be Irish."

"Her grandfather was from Dublin. I inherited his coloring."

"Ah. I'll bet my mom has had more husbands and boyfriends than yours."

"You win hands down. My mother isn't into guys. She's a lesbian."

Her eyes widened a fraction. "Oh."

"Yeah. She told Dad she'd fallen out of love with him, but he never guessed she was gay. He didn't find out until she filed divorce papers a couple months later." By then, she'd finally dropped her phony facade, trading makeup and feminine clothes for overalls, wife-beater shirts and hiking boots. "Shocked the hell out of him and Aunt Polly. He fell apart."

"I can't even imagine."

She had no idea. Gus had tried to be the adult, not easy for a seven-year-old with a poor grasp of the situation. To make matters worse, his mother had moved to San Francisco and turned her back on him. She'd waited twelve years, until around the time Gus had started working at the fire department, to contact him. They kept in touch, but not regularly.

"I wanted to fix things and make my dad happy again, but I didn't know how," he added.

"Of course not. How could anyone fix someone else's marriage? I hope he met someone else."

"He's dated over the years but nothing that lasted." Gus wished something would stick, but who was he to criticize, when his relationships were just as short-lived?

"What about your dad?" he asked. "Do you have a stepmom?"

"Who knows? Once he left, I never heard from him."

"Bummer." At least he spoke with his mom from time to time.

"His loss. So how old were you when you and your dad went to live with Polly?"

Gus wide-eyed her. "She told you about that, huh?"

"Not the specifics, only that you grew up in her house."

His childhood was no secret, but he couldn't help wondering what else she'd shared with Wanda. "We moved in when my mother filed for divorce. Aunt Polly was in her fifties then, and the head librarian at the Guff's Lake Library. She gave up the position and switched to part-time so she could raise me. Back then, Dad was a lieutenant at the fire station. He made good money, enough to support us."

Wanda nodded, then checked her phone for the time. "It's getting late, and I need to use the bathroom."

Gus glanced at his watch, surprised to see that nearly an hour had passed since she'd arrived.

She stood. "When I get back, you can tell me about Polly."

~

STANDING AT THE RESTROOM SINK, Wanda freshened her lipstick. Then frowned at her reflection. Without contacts, eyeliner or fake lashes, she looked so much plainer and duller.

No wonder Gus had noticed. She dug for the makeup kit in her handbag but changed her mind. Fixing herself up took time, and she'd already kept him waiting once this morning.

Besides, in his company, she could relax and have a conversation without flirting or pretending to be the life of the party. Although for a few seconds there, she'd thought sure Gus expected her to be that woman.

But he'd told her to be herself—a suggestion she couldn't remember ever hearing before. Shedding her fake persona felt strange but hadn't been as difficult as she'd expected. Mainly because Gus seemed interested in whatever she said, even the dull stuff. He even asked questions. Most guys wanted to talk about themselves.

They would be friends, she decided—platonic friends. A girl didn't need to fancy herself up for that.

With a sense of relief, she returned to the table. Gus had two fresh coffees waiting.

She didn't have to force a delighted smile. "How did you know I needed a refill?"

"Lucky guess. Let's talk about Aunt Polly and her refusal to downsize and move into a retirement community."

"Because, as we already agreed, she's a proud, independent woman."

"And stubborn as they come."

"When I grew up, I lived in numerous apartments in Tillamook. I've never owned a house, but I can imagine how difficult it must be to let go of the place she's called home all these years." Wanda rubbed the area above her heart, which ached a little for Gus's poor aunt.

"Especially her place. Her husband, my great uncle Martin, was a successful local architect. He designed and built it for their tenth anniversary."

"Nice gift."

Gus nodded. "After a decade of trying to have kids and failing, they still hoped for a miracle. With that in mind, he designed their home with four bedrooms— one on the main floor and three upstairs."

"That's a lot of house for one elderly woman. No wonder you want her to move."

"She doesn't even go upstairs anymore. The property isn't in great shape, either. It needs work, but she isn't interested. Partly because of finances, and partly because she's comfortable as is."

Wanda finished her scone and sucked the butter off her thumb. The light that sparked in Gus's eyes set off a responding zing she felt clear to her toes. If she didn't know better, she'd think he wanted a kiss.

Her wayward lips actually tingled.

Dropping her gaze, she fiddled with the paper doily on her empty plate. Even if she wanted to kiss him, she wouldn't, not if she intended to stick with her plan. She hadn't flirted or encouraged him in any way. He couldn't possibly be interested in the plain-vanilla version of herself.

Ignoring the unwanted physical reactions, she continued with the subject at hand. "All those bedrooms, and she never did have any kids," she said, again hurting for the woman.

"A real shame," Gus agreed. "Aunt Polly was made to raise a bunch of kids. Even at fifty-four, she was a better mom to me than my biological mother ever was."

"You lucked out. Why didn't they adopt?"

"She's never said. The story gets even sadder. Two years after they moved in, Uncle Martin suffered a brain hemorrhage and died." Gus shook his head. "He was fifty-two, thirteen years older than Aunt Polly. His death made her a widow at thirty-nine."

Wanda gave her head a sorrowful shake. "To lose your husband at such a young age... The poor woman has been through a lot."

"It happened before my time, but my dad remembers she was devastated, but put up a good front. Like she does now. At least Uncle Martin left her fairly well-off, so she was able to pay off the mortgage and buy things she couldn't afford on her salary."

"Didn't you say she can't afford to fix up the house?"

"I did. After forty years, that money is gone. She lives off her library pension and social security. Anyway, she had plenty of room for me and my dad."

"She never remarried?"

Gus shook his head. "She was fifty-four when we moved in. She claimed taking care of us was all the family she needed."

"So your moving in was good for both you and her. Still, widowed that young and never falling in love again... That's tragic."

"She's a survivor. As much as she loves the house, she needs to pare down and move to a place where she doesn't have to worry about home maintenance or a yard. Plus, if she should suffer another stroke..." Gus swallowed hard. "She should live in a place with people nearby to help."

That made sense. Wanda glanced at her phone again. "I have a noon cut and color. I should leave soon, and I still don't know why I'm here."

With a solemn expression, Gus canted toward her, as if what he was about to say was extremely important. "Aunt Polly won't listen to me, my dad, or any of the guys I work with. But she listens to you."

"Me?" Realizing her jaw had dropped, Wanda quickly shut her mouth. "You want me to convince your aunt Polly to sell her house and move into a retirement community."

"I knew you'd get it."

"Hold on, Gus. I style her hair once a week, but I really don't know her that well. And there's the age difference. I'm twenty-eight and she's old enough to be my great grandma. I don't see how I can possibly have any influence on her."

"She's always talking about how special you are. Will you give it whirl?"

The last thing Wanda wanted was to step in between Gus and his great aunt. Especially in a matter that had nothing to do with her and would likely upset Polly. She snorted. "You don't ask for much, do you?"

"You're my best bet. Please."

What sane woman could resist those warm, pleading baby greens? She sighed. "When do you want me to do this, and what exactly should I say?"

He exhaled loudly, as if he'd been holding his breath. "As soon as possible. Try whatever you think will work."

"Gee, that's a big help. Okay, but I think I'd have better luck lassoing the moon."

6

If anyone could get Aunt Polly to think seriously about moving, Wanda could. Hopeful for the first time in weeks, Gus slipped on his Ray-Bans and escorted her out of the Coffee Shack.

As the door shut behind them, she stiffened. "That's Betty Randall," she muttered, nodding at the gray-haired woman exiting a Ford. "Aka gossip central, and Carole Sue's mainline to other people's business. God only knows what she'll say about running into us, together out here."

She donned her own shades—as if that could mask her identity.

Gus had seen Betty in action on the day Sam's son, William, had gone missing. As concerned and caring as she'd been that afternoon, she'd wasted no time spreading the news of Adam and Sam's romance. The last thing he wanted was for her to speculate all over town about him and Wanda.

"C'mon." He took Wanda's arm and steered her around the building, out of the blabbermouth's sight range.

Hurrying to keep up, Wanda giggled for the first time today, a tinkling sound he enjoyed.

"You're clever," she said, sounding breathless.

He grinned. "That goes without saying."

They dashed around the corner to the back, where they were less likely to be noticed. Wanting to see Wanda's eyes, he slid his sunglasses to the top of his head and removed hers.

"Hey," she said, as he pocketed them. "What did you do that for?"

"We're on the shaded side where we don't need them. Don't worry, you'll get them back. What do you think she's doing so far out of town?"

"Gathering intel? This place is really close to Guff's Lake, where a lot of romantic stuff happens. I'll bet she stops by for coffee and gossip."

"Are you referring to the old myth that when a couple kisses under the big ash tree at the lake, they'll find true and lasting love?" Gus snorted.

"You don't believe it?" Wanda's purple lips pursed a fraction.

Mesmerized, he shook his head. "It's just a story invented to bring lovers out here, in hopes they spend money."

"What a cynical thing to say."

"Don't tell me you believe the hype."

"I've never kissed anyone there, and no one I know has, either, but I like the romance of it." She gave him a dirty look. "You're doing it again. Staring at my mouth."

"It's a very sexy mouth, even when you frown."

Her eyes widened as if she hadn't expected this. "It is?"

He nodded. "I like you better when you smile." With his fingers, he gently prodded the corners of her lips upward, but as soon as he let go, they flattened out again. "Have it your way. FYI, you look amazing without the fake lashes and colored contact lenses."

"Don't lie to me, Gus. My natural eye color is dull as dirt, and my lashes are too short."

"I wouldn't lie. Brown eyes, with green and gold flecks...very attractive."

"Attractive," she repeated, sounding skeptical.

She didn't seem to think much of her looks, but he was too distracted to wonder at that.

"Uh-huh." Hands on either side of her head, he leaned in nice and close. "You smell like summer flowers."

"It's the lavender shampoo." Furrows lined her normally-smooth forehead. "What are you doing, Gus?"

"Getting ready to kiss you."

She raised her chin, no doubt to tell him to knock it off. He smiled into those eyes and they lost their *back-off* spark.

Seconds later, her eyelids dropped to half-mast in a clear go-ahead. So he did.

One brief brush of his mouth over those soft, welcoming lips wasn't enough. Cupping her face he went in for more, this time sliding his tongue along the seam of her mouth. She let him in. He tasted coffee, blueberry scone and something all her own.

She slid her palms up his chest and...shoved him away?

"Don't, Gus."

Hands up, he stepped back.

"I'm taking a break from men," she said.

"That's right. After Larry." Gus silently cursed the bastard for fouling up what he wanted more of. "What did he do, anyway?"

"He was just the latest in a long string of bad relationships. I don't have much luck with men, and I need to figure out why."

Gus nodded. "You're preaching to the choir here."

"Have you figured out the reason it keeps happening?"

"Things don't work out," he said, shrugging. "What more is there to know?"

"If you figure out the why of your problems with women, you might have better luck next time. Hand over my sunglasses. I have to go."

As soon as Wanda slid her shades into place, she headed at a brisk clip around the building. Gus stayed right with her.

"You don't need to run," he said. "I won't bite."

"I'm trying to arrive at the salon ahead of my noon appointme—"

They almost collided with Betty Randall.

The woman had been making her way to the door all this time? Damn. She moved slower than Aunt Polly.

She stopped smack in their path. "Well, hello, Wanda and Gus."

Judging by her wily grin, she was already making up a story to broadcast. He gave a curt nod. "Hey, Betty."

"Hi," Wanda chimed in.

"Fancy running into you two all the way out here. One would think you didn't want people to see you together. If that's the case, you ought to wipe that purple lipstick off your face, Gus."

Wanda's eyebrows shot up. She touched the corner of her lip with her little finger. Gus rubbed the corresponding place on his mouth with his knuckle, and she gave a covert nod.

"We had a meeting," she explained to Betty.

"It seems to have been very productive. Bye, you two." Looking like the proverbial cat that swallowed the canary, she broke speed limits getting through the front door, proving she could move quickly when she wanted.

Wanda groaned. "She already has her cell phone in hand."

This was not good. "She's right about one thing. I asked to meet out here because I wanted to avoid running into people I know. I don't want Aunt Polly to find out you and I talked about her, or to get any cock-eyed ideas about us."

"If she does, I'll set her and everyone else straight. I don't want people thinking my break from men is over."

With most of the purple gone from her lips and her hair on the messy side, she looked the opposite—thoroughly kissed. Red-blooded male that he was, he considered going in for more.

But Betty Randall was probably watching from the window. Gus shoved his hands in his jeans pockets. "Then why did you kiss me?"

"*You* kissed *me*."

Like that explained her warm response.

"We have to make sure everyone knows this morning was strictly a friend thing," she went on.

With Aunt Polly in mind, Gus agreed. "One friend helping another." He scratched his head. "What are we helping each other with?"

"Polly, remember? But you don't want her to find out, so we won't mention that. I know—our problems with the opposite sex." She checked the screen on her phone and frowned. "If I don't leave immediately, I'll be late for my twelve o'clock. Thanks for the scone and coffee."

"Thanks for agreeing to help. And for those kisses," he added.

She blushed. "Bye, Gus."

She almost ran toward her car, as if she couldn't get away from him fast enough.

THE FOLLOWING day at zero eight hundred sharp—military time—Gus joined the rest of the crew in the firehouse kitchen for breakfast, around the large table that doubled as a place to play cards and board games during slow times. While on duty, they took all meals together, and punctuality was a given. Breakfast at eight, lunch at noon, dinner at eighteen hundred. With the exception of dinner, which crew members took turns cooking and serving, the guys provided and prepared their own food.

After breakfast, Captain Comings held at meeting one floor down in the apparatus bay, also known as the garage. As soon as the crew gathered in the space between the fire engines and aid cars, the captain reviewed the day ahead so all crew members knew everyone's agendas.

Last month Gus had divided his job between paramedic duties and updating the safety project. This month was split between fighting fires and the project, with today earmarked for inspections.

"How many inspections do you have scheduled for today?" Captain Comings asked.

"Four before lunch, four this afternoon."

"That's a tall order."

"I intend to finish the western quadrant today." The fire department had divided Guff's Lake into four sections—north, south, east and west—with the west quadrant containing the highest density of commercial businesses and apartment complexes.

Captain Comings nodded. "You're making decent progress."

"Slow, but steady." Too slow. Finishing by the first of August would be tough. On the plus side, inspections in the other quadrants shouldn't take as long.

"Let's snap to, men," the captain said.

While Gus changed into his shirt with the safety inspection logo and other crew members took care of their tasks, Rafe, who Gus had worked with for eleven years, wandered over.

"Tommie's Hair and Nails this afternoon, huh. I heard about you and one of the hairstylists. Wanda something."

Gus wasn't surprised. Four days had passed since he'd kissed Wanda, giving old Betty Randall plenty of time to spread the story. "Lipmann. What did you hear?" he asked, wondering what tales she'd spun.

Several other crewmates joined the conversation.

"Last week you were seen together at the Coffee Shack," Rafe said. "With her lipstick on your face."

Side-stepping that red-hot fact, Gus segued to his reason for meeting up with Wanda. "She does Aunt Polly's hair. They get along real well. Keep this to yourself, but I asked her to help convince my aunt it's time to move. Because I'm sure not having any luck on my own. Ask Owen and Max. They were at lunch the other day."

Both men nodded.

"Why didn't you meet Wanda in town and save yourself time and gas?" Hank, the department's newest recruit, asked.

"I didn't want people telling Aunt Polly they'd seen us together. I don't want her to find out we're talking about her or getting the idea we're interested in each other."

"Too late for that." Rafe grinned. The station's former stud-in-residence had recently traded his roving eye for the love of one woman, Jillian, but he got his jollies razzing the rest of them.

"Look, Wanda and I are friends," Gus explained. "She talked about her relationship problems."

"Before or after the kiss?"

Gus didn't answer that.

"Did you discuss your problems with women?" Owen asked.

"Some."

"And she still kissed you?"

Rafe hooted. Gus tried to stare the joker down but failed. "Don't you need to call Jillian before things get hectic around here?"

Remarkably cheerful, Rafe widened his grin. "We said our good-byes in bed this morning. Your aunt Polly's gonna be pleased about you and Wanda."

"So far, she hasn't brought it up. Could be, no one has told her." A guy could hope. "She'd better not hear anything from you or anyone else in this room." Gus made sure his level look included them all.

Owen shook his head. "Like you can keep her from finding out."

Aunt Polly did enjoy gossip. "If she does, it won't change anything," Gus said. "Wanda's taking a break from men. She's had her heart broken a lot."

He'd been hurt, too, because splitting up always hurt—even though he usually initiated the breakup. He didn't want to be responsible for one more.

"Who says she's going to fall for you?" Owen asked. "As long as she doesn't, she won't get hurt."

"I can't explain her reasoning, and I'd bet my right

leg neither can anyone else here. None of us really understand how women think." Gus nodded at Captain Comings, who'd been married more than twenty years, and Rafe and Adam, both in solid relationships. "Not even you three."

"You got me there," Rafe said. "Jillian and I are tight. We talk about everything, but I'll never understand how her mind works."

Adam nodded. "I want Sam to be happy. That's the main thing."

"Smart man," the captain chimed in. "When Audrey is happy, I'm happy."

The crew dispersed until only Owen remained.

"I know you, bro," he said. "You like this woman."

"There is something about her," Gus admitted. "But she has her plan, and she's determined to stick to it."

"What a downer."

"Not really. I'm not that into her. As I said the other day, she's not my type."

Even so, he couldn't stop thinking about the taste of her luscious mouth, so warm and eager against his. And those soft curves pressed close...

"Will you see her at Tommie's today?" Owen asked.

"Yep. The salon is closed Mondays, but she'll be there to let me in."

Just him and her, alone together.

His body started to rev up. With grim determination, he shut it down. As much as he'd enjoyed those kisses, he wasn't going there again. Period. Wanda wasn't the woman for him.

Today was about finishing the western quadrant, getting through one inspection and moving on to the next.

He grabbed his stuff and headed out.

Not wanting to keep Gus waiting a second time, Wanda intended to be at the salon by one o'clock.

Unfortunately, she arrived ten minutes late.

And there he was, one broad shoulder against the front door, in a dark blue shirt and pants. The shirt fit him well and highlighted his solid chest and flat belly, and the pants hinted at his powerful legs.

It was a miracle she didn't swoon.

"Hi," she said, squinting against the bright sun as she hurried toward him. "Have you been here long?"

"Not half as long as the other day."

No teasing smile accompanied the quip, underscoring a low tolerance for tardiness. Wanda wasn't about to explain that she'd been fighting with herself over whether or not to put on eyelashes and colored contact lenses. Gus preferred her eyes natural.

In the end, to prove she wasn't wavering on her decision to take a break from men and wasn't trying to please him, she'd gone with the lashes and copper-tinted contacts, giving her eyes a dramatic jeweled look.

He hefted a rectangular briefcase from the pavement beside him.

"Yes, sir. You're grumpy today."

"You're the first of four appointments this afternoon, and I'd like to arrive at the rest on time."

"I apologize for not being here at one on the dot," she said, trying not to sound pissy. After all, this was her fault. "Wait here while I disengage the alarm."

She stepped through the door. The salon always felt strange when there was no one else inside— empty and way too quiet. After taking care of the alarm, she hit the lights, which helped, and then cued up a Sade CD. She set the volume low enough that the singer's mellow music provided background without drowning out conversation. At last, the place felt bright and welcoming.

Returning to the entrance, she gestured Gus inside.

By his black expression and the tension radiating from him, he was still steamed about something.

Wanda sighed. "What is it this time?"

"You're not taking our appointment seriously. You should. It's important, both for the Guff's Lake Fire Department and this salon."

"I said I was sorry!"

What had gotten into her? She never yelled, especially at a man. Contrite, she bit her lip. Which unlike her eyes, she'd left au naturel, so he wouldn't stare at her mouth.

Now she was tense. Not even Sade's soothing voice helped.

Gus looked startled by her outburst. "Hey, I'm not mad at you. It's the damn gossip. The whole crew knows about the other day."

Lovely. Wanda sighed. "If the guys at the station know, everyone at the salon will, too." Imagining the speculative looks when the salon opened in the morning, she cringed. How in the world would she explain about being with Gus at the Coffee Shack? She didn't want people thinking she'd abandoned her plan. She groaned. "We've been expecting this. Still, I'd like to wring Betty Randall's neck."

"Get in line."

She gestured around. "I'll leave you alone while you do your thing." A little space might help them both calm down. "If you need anything, I'll be in the office, straight through the Employees Only door."

There was nothing to do back there, but anything was better than hanging around Gus.

"Better stick around to show me where the smoke and fire alarms are and to point out all exits in the building."

So much for regaining her composure. "All right. We may as well start in this area."

Gus set his case down, clicked the fastenings open and pulled out an iPad. Keeping the meeting on a professional level, she pivoted away and strode forward. She felt his eyes on her and fought to keep her hips from swaying. She'd dressed down today, in jeans, an oversize T-shirt and flats. If Cindy knew, she'd have fits, but Wanda wanted to make a point.

Anything to keep him from looking at her like he did at the Coffee Shack. As if he wanted to eat her up. Never mind that after those kisses the other day, she wanted him to do exactly that.

No. She didn't. *I'm taking a break*, she firmly reminded herself.

For all the good that did. She still wanted more with Gus. If she flirted enough, he'd ask her out. Then they might get involved, and whatever was good between them would quickly sour. It always did.

Wanda didn't want that to happen. She wanted to be comfortable around Gus, be his friend. In other words, stick with the plan. Her mantra from this moment on.

They wandered around the salon and she pointed out the exits, alarms and sprinklers. Gus marked them on an e-blueprint of the salon. He also checked to ensure each was in working condition, and typed in notes.

While his head bent toward the device she was free to study him. His strong, sturdy neck and the tiny mole at his hairline. His sleeves, rolled up at the cuffs. She'd always had a thing about a man's forearms, and his ranked right up there at the top. Thick and slightly tanned, with a smattering of hair, and the masculine watch that looked especially sexy... *Whew*.

Quit looking at him, she silently chided. She frowned at her nails, noting a chip in one. She could always schedule a manicure with Betty Jo, the manicurist, but she didn't want to show up at work tomorrow with her nails like this.

She glanced up to find Gus staring at her. "Do you need something?"

"Nope." His expression unreadable, he tapped something on the iPad.

They headed through the Employees Only door, into the kitchen and checked the last of the alarms and sprinklers.

"You passed inspection," he said.

"Tommie will be glad."

After signing and dating two certificates of safety compliance, he snapped photos for his records and then handed her the originals. "Be sure to replace the old certificates with these."

"I'll do that while you're here."

After taking care of the one in the kitchen, she carried the other into the salon. "I've been thinking about how to talk to Polly," she said as she tacked it to the wall. "I'll start by inviting her out for coffee."

Gus shook his head. "She doesn't like to go out for coffee."

"I know she likes to eat lunch out. I'll set up a lunch date."

He didn't look any more pleased. In the interest of getting along, Wanda hid her frustration. "What do you suggest?"

"That's up to you."

What was the deal? She gave him a sideways look. "You've changed your mind about me talking to her."

Not wanting to butt in where she didn't belong in the first place, she should have been pleased. Instead, she was hurt. Which made about as much sense as a heat wave in January. "Why didn't you just tell me, Gus?"

He seemed genuinely surprised. "Where'd you get that idea? I need you to talk to her."

"Gee, I don't know. Could it be because you've done nothing but frown and bark at me since I gave up my afternoon off to meet you here?"

He scrubbed his hand over his face. "Look, I'm trying to keep this on a strictly-business level."

Wasn't that what they were doing?

"The thing is, I keep thinking about kissing you again." His gaze dropped to her mouth.

So much for the sloppy outfit and skipping the lipstick today.

All the nerves in her body hummed. "You caught me by surprise the other day," she explained.

Which hadn't stopped her from savoring every moment in his arms. From his warm hands, tenderly cupping her face, to the heady heat of his tongue exploring her mouth. He was an excellent kisser, a good indicator he'd be an equally fine lover.

The truth was, from the second she'd opened her eyes this morning, she'd thought about a repeat of the other day.

"You handle yourself very well when surprised."

The corners of his lips quirked, charming her. She fought to remember how easily her heart bruised. For her own good, the relationship with Gus stopped at friendship, period.

Stick with the plan.

"You don't want to kiss this." She gestured from her head to her flats. In drab clothing and little makeup, she was plain as a white paper plate. "Maybe you need glasses."

"My vision is twenty-twenty, and the way you look today, you're hard to resist."

"If you expect me to believe that—"

"I wouldn't lie."

She couldn't believe her ears. Every guy she'd met gravitated toward the carefully made up, colorful, sexy version of herself she played so well. Gus was pulling her leg.

Although he seemed sincere. Was it possible he liked the real her?

Something buried so deep inside, Wanda hadn't realized it was there, unfurled and rejoiced. She wanted to melt. Did.

Then and there, she gave him a little piece of her heart. She couldn't help it.

Her face must have betrayed some of her feelings, for Gus's grin faded into somber intensity. He pinned her with his hungry eyes, rendering her helpless to glance away. She recognized that hot look from the other day, just before he'd kissed her.

Yes! Every molecule in her body strained toward him with its own level of hunger. Lacing her fingers together to keep from reaching for him, she lowered her gaze from those mesmerizing eyes to his chest.

Big mistake. She knew the feel of that solid torso pressed warmly against her breasts....

Wanda cleared her throat and raised her eyes. "Back to Polly. Wednesday, I'll ask if she wants to get together, and let her pick the time and place."

"She'll like that."

His eyes never left hers, and his expression remained intent. Resisting him wasn't easy. "I like you, Gus, and I'm attracted to you. But I think we should be friends and nothing more."

Her brain believed every word. Her body, not so much.

"I'm okay with that. It's probably best for both of us."

"I won't keep you," she said, afraid if he didn't leave, she'd have a change of heart, do something foolish and jump his bones. In an effort to remain strong, she twined her fingers together at her waist. "I know you have visits scheduled at other buildings."

He nodded. With a potent look that frayed the last remnants of her willpower, he started toward her.

Dear God, she wanted him to kiss her. Ached for him. She dropped her hands to her sides and stood waiting. Instead of putting her out of her misery, he strode to his case, picked it up and made for the door.

"Gus," she pleaded, helpless against her desire.

His back to her, he stopped. "What?"

"I need... I want... That is..."

"Don't say it," he cautioned in a low growl.

"That I changed my mind and want to kiss you?"

"That's not a good idea." Despite his words, he set down the case.

"Please."

He made a sound of pure male hunger and pivoted around. From his smoldering expression to the caged hunger of his massive body as he closed the space between them, everything about him screamed passion. Danger.

Don't do this. Don't set yourself up for trouble later, she advised herself. She reached for him anyway.

Gus and only Gus filled her senses. The clean scent of soap and man. Muscled arms, lifting her so that her eyes were level with his. Eager lips and the taste of his passion. She lost herself in deep, shuddering kisses, felt his arousal against his hip.

From somewhere, a moan filled the air. Her own, she dimly realized.

Wanting him, she wriggled closer. Or tried. To her frustration, he suddenly broke away.

Breathing hard, he rested his forehead against hers. "Wanda."

"Hmmm?"

"Aren't you supposed to be taking a break from guys?"

She tried to think about that but couldn't. In the heat of the moment, she didn't want to. "We're not dating, so this doesn't count," she rationalized.

Unable to bear the distance between his mouth and hers, she pulled him down for another kiss. Or tried. The stubborn brute refused to budge.

"You're not making any sense."

"Who cares?" She rose up and pressed her lips to his.

8

———

If Gus was smart, he'd pull away from Wanda for good and put a stop to what they were doing. The thought flitted through his mind. Then she pressed her sweet curves up against him and sucked his tongue, and his brain fogged up.

He needed to put his hands on her. Without breaking the kiss, he backed up toward the sofa in the waiting area. Moments later, she lay across it, the padded arm cushioning her head.

Too big to lie with her on the thing, he leaned down and took her mouth. More mind-numbing kisses followed. He cupped her breasts through the T-shirt and teased her nipples to sharp peaks. Moaning, she arched up into his palms.

He wanted her. Naked, writhing under him. Now.

The instant he lifted the hem of her shirt, she stiffened. "No, Gus."

When he dropped his hands, she scrambled to a sitting position. He slid over, putting much-needed space between them. "Got a little carried away," he said, scrubbing his hand over his face.

No kidding. Was he nuts? He silently swore.

He never messed around on the job, let alone with

tight time constraints. Worse still, Wanda didn't seem to know who she really was or what she wanted. If that wasn't a recipe for trouble...

Gus didn't want to get involved with her. But when her hazel eyes went soft with longing and her provocative mouth plumped into kiss mode, his desire for her drowned out all else.

She fussed with her hair, caught her pink bottom lip between her teeth, and stood. "You're going to be late to your next appointment."

Gus also rose. "Not if I leave right immediately."

She didn't say another word. Her silence worried him almost as much as his errant conduct.

"Look, we didn't plan on that happening, but it did," he said as they reached the door. "We didn't do anything wrong."

Except ignite the smoking volcano inside him.

"It's just..." She hesitated, then shook her head. "Never mind."

Gus wanted to hear what she had to say, but he didn't have time. "We ought to talk about this, and I promise we will. Soon."

"Or we could just forget it ever happened."

"I don't think that's possible, Wanda."

To make a point, he tipped up her chin and dragged his mouth over hers. Her eyes closed and didn't open again until he grabbed his case. She slid the deadbolt back and opened the door.

He left.

~

GIVING herself a swift mental kick in the butt, Wanda sank against the wall. What had gotten into her?

Gus was supposed to be her friend, not the man

she kissed with abandon and lusted after. She wasn't supposed to do those things with him or any other man right now.

Yet she'd thrown caution to the winds. All because, puzzling as it was, he seemed to want her. Even at her plainest, most drab self, the self she hid from every male in sight and most customers.

For that alone, she was already half in love with him.

Wanda frowned. Darn it, she was doing it again, following her usual pattern of getting suckered into love way too fast. A pattern for which she always paid heavy consequences.

Take today. One warm look, one genuine compliment, and she'd become putty in Gus's hands. His very capable hands...

Her barely banked hunger flared, making her dizzy with desire. Irritated with herself, she marched to the stereo and shut off the music. At least she'd stopped before things had gone too far. Which had taken every ounce of strength she possessed, but she couldn't afford to lose herself in heat of the moment. Especially when, despite Gus's melting expression and claim to like the unvarnished her, a little part of her doubted his sincerity.

Did he want her for herself or just for sex?

She enjoyed sex and knew how to please a man. But what about the more important wants and needs buried beneath the passion? When a relationship was based on sex, sooner or later—usually sooner in her experience—the passion and the relationship died.

If she gave into her physical yearning and jumped straight into sex, how would she ever figure out what any guy, what Gus, truly wanted?

She'd vowed not to get involved until she solved

that million-dollar question. Then what was she doing, fantasizing about a man she could easily give her
heart to?

Wanda refused to let that happen. She flipped the
lights off and raised her chin. As of this second, she
would change. Would not be attracted to Gus Viggio
or think about him as anything but a friend. She
would help him convince Polly to consider living in a
retirement community, but that was it.

Filled with resolve, she reset the alarm, stepped
outside, and locked the door. Slipping on sunglasses,
she headed purposefully for her car.

The cobalt blue Civic sparkled in the sun, like a
cheerleader rooting her on for sticking to her guns.

But even with her firm words and pep talk, all she
could think of was seeing Gus again.

9

A t dinner Monday night, Adam cooked up a huge pan of beef and rice that smelled great. His belly empty, Gus helped himself. He passed the pan to Owen, and then piled salad and a couple slices of bread on his plate. As soon as the last man at the table dished up, everyone dug in.

Moments into the meal, Rafe nodded at Gus from across the table. "So you and Wanda, alone at Tommie's. How'd that go?"

He would bring that up. Gus didn't bother to glance up from his food. "The inspection went well."

"Of Wanda or the building?"

His fork clattered against the plate. "What's that supposed to mean?"

Gus's bud toyed with a grin. "Just asking."

He shrugged and picked up the fork. "I got what I went in for."

Loud hoots all around.

"You guys are a barrel of laughs," he muttered.

Little did they know he'd gotten a whole lot more than he'd ever imagined. Hours had passed, but thinking about making out with Wanda turned him on—and also pissed him off. Dammit, he knew better.

"While I worked my ass off to finish the western quadrant, did I miss any action here?"

The conversation turned to an apartment fire the team had put out earlier and then to stuff Gus tuned out.

Now that he'd sampled Wanda's hunger, he wanted more. He wanted to make her cry out and lose herself in pleasure. Under him, on top, every which way... Even if he knew better.

The comment about him not wanting to kiss her simply because she wore her grubs underscored that she thought herself unattractive unless she dressed in fancy clothes and heavy makeup. He wanted a woman who didn't have to hide behind props, s woman comfortable with herself as is.

"...Poker game at my house Friday night," Max was saying. "You coming, Gus?"

The standing poker game happened Friday nights and rotated among crewmembers, with anyone from the department welcome. Gus hadn't been in weeks. "If it wasn't for that Lincoln, I would."

Max's lips twitched. "I think you're worried I'll beat your ass and take all your money."

Rob winked. "If it were me, I'd ditch the car and work on Wanda Lipmann. Since you're not interested, maybe I'll give her a call."

Gus narrowed his eyes. "Stay away from her."

"Get a load of this guy." Rob elbowed Hank. "He likes her, all right."

"I'd bet money on it," Hank agreed.

Gus helped himself to more bread. "Seriously, I need to work on the Lincoln."

"How's that going?" the captain asked.

"She's a honey of a car, or will be when I finish with her. I'm still scouting around for parts. I'll post before-and-after photos on my website like I always do."

Guys started in with questions and comments, and the rest of the meal passed without a hitch.

Later, after Gus did his evening chores and prepped for possible calls during the night, he holed up in the little room where he bunked. Sitting on the simple frame bed, he phoned Wanda.

"Gus." She sounded surprised and a little flustered. "Hi."

Smiling, he leaned against the wall. He heard something that sounded like covers. "What's that rustling noise? You in bed?"

He pictured her in an oversize T-shirt like the one she'd worn today, wearing nothing underneath. In a snap he was rock-hard.

"At nine o'clock? There are days when I wish I could fall asleep early, but I'm not wired that way. I'll be up for hours yet. I'm sitting on the balcony with a glass of wine, enjoying the evening."

"Nice. But it's early spring and not exactly warm outside. Aren't you cold?"

"I wrapped up in an old blanket and I'm toasty. What's going on? Is Polly okay?"

"She's fine. So you're relaxing on your balcony." Gus's tiny apartment didn't have room for that. Between his salary and the money he earned from the car restoration business, he could easily afford a house with a big deck. With no one but himself to think about, he didn't see the point. "What part of town are you in?"

"The west side, not far from the salon. My apartment is on the seventh floor. Near enough to the ground that I hear noises from the street, but high enough to give me a sense of peace. The balcony is too small for real patio furniture, but the great view more than makes up for that. On a clear day, I can see the Siskiyou Mountains."

"You can't see anything at night."

"What about the stars? With the moon barely a sliver, they're spectacular."

"It's been awhile since I spent much time looking at the night sky, but as a kid I did a lot of stargazing. I used to lie on the grass at Aunt Polly's and stare up for hours." Focusing on the sky had helped him shut out the turmoil and emptiness his mother had left in her wake.

"We didn't have a yard, but I pulled a chair up to my bedroom window and looked out. I was always on the lookout for shooting stars to wish on."

"What did you wish for?" he asked.

"Mostly shallow stuff—that I was taller and thinner and more popular."

He laughed softly. "I can match you for shallow. When I hit puberty, my big wish was for certain girls to let me fool around with them."

She made a sound that could be humorous or scornful. "You guys are all alike. I look at more than the stars. There are bunches of nice homes nearby, some all lit up at night. My favorite is a two-story with lots of windows. It's fun to imagine the family inside."

"What do they look like?"

"I couldn't say. I've never met them."

"In your imagination."

"Well, there's a mother, a father and a couple of kids. Also a dog and a cat. They're a warm, happy family, sharing what they did during the day and laughing often."

Her wistful tone spoke volumes.

"I came from a family like that," Gus said. "The

happy part—we didn't have a big house. That was before my mom figured out she was a lesbian."

"At least you have good memories of your early childhood."

"You probably do, too."

"There were times when Cindy, Crystal and I had fun together. Ages ago." She exhaled loudly.

"You don't live in the same town anymore."

"We're three-hundred-odd miles apart, so I can't just drive over there for an hour or two. Plus, we're all so busy. And my mother—a little of her goes a long way."

"I hear that. My mom lives in San Francisco, and I rarely see her. Occasionally we touch base by phone or email. Works great for me." Gus propped his arm behind his head. "If you're on the west side, I inspected your apartment building. What's the address?" She gave it to him, and he shook his head. "No way— that was my last inspection before lunch."

"Seriously? I didn't see you on the premises, but then I was in my apartment. Did we pass?"

"Yep."

"Hooray. You never said why you called."

Gus cleared his throat. "We didn't get to finish our conversation this afternoon. We're okay, right?"

He didn't want to get involved with her, but he didn't want her mad at him, either.

"Since you brought up the subject..." She paused. "What we did shouldn't happen again."

They were on the same wavelength, which was good.

"I agree. I like you, but we don't need to be fooling around. I'm not looking for a relationship, and you have your plan."

"That's good to know, and a big relief."

"I also have a plan—to finish that Lincoln I told you about."

"You enjoy working on classic cars. I can tell by the tone of your voice."

"Wouldn't do it if I didn't. Hey, would you like to see her?" The second he uttered the question, he shut his mouth. Had he just invited Wanda to the garage?

"The Lincoln is a she?"

She laughed, a melodic sound that drew out his own chuckle. "Yeah, but don't ask me why. She seems to fit. I'll be working on the engine later in the week."

"I'm tempted." She hesitated. "I don't know, Gus. We just agreed we don't want to start anything, but this sounds an awful lot like a date."

"I'd never bring a date to the garage. You like classic cars, and this one is pretty cool. Even when she's in rough shape. If you're interested, I could use an extra pair of hands."

"But I know nothing about car engines. Even if I did, I really don't have time to help out."

"No prob." Gus should have been fine with that, not disappointed. But now that he'd offered to show her around the garage, he wanted to her to see it. Never mind why—he just did. He sat up and thought about turning in.

"I would like to get a look at her, though," Wanda added, and Gus's world brightened way too much. "How about before work Thursday or Friday?"

"Let's aim for Thursday. You can fill me in on the plans you and Aunt Polly made to get together." No doubt, his aunt would do the same when he picked her up from the salon, but he wanted Wanda's take.

"Thursday it is. Where should we meet?"

"I'll pick you up at your place at nine-thirty."

"I'd rather drive myself."

She really was playing safe, but her way felt more like casual friends. Fine by him.

"Sure." He gave her driving directions. "It's a garage. I wouldn't dress up."

"Then I'll need to go home and change in time for work."

"Looking around won't take long."

"We have a date," she said, before hastening to clarify. "Not a real date. The 'I'll put it on the calendar' kind."

Gus grinned, but he couldn't have said why.

MID-MORNING WEDNESDAY, Wanda styled a customer's hair with an eye on the door. Any minute, Gus would escort Polly in for her weekly appointment.

Wanda was a little tense, even had butterflies in her stomach. Nerves associated with the upcoming conversation with Polly, she assured herself. Nothing to do with seeing Gus.

Her customer paid and left. Rather than head to the kitchen to relax for a few minutes, she stayed at her station.

Tommie, working two stations over, flashed a smile. "Love the black-and-gold pixilated designs in your hair today."

She wore her hair short and uncolored—straight, brown and streaked with gray. Yet she liked everything Wanda did to hers.

Tommie's customer, a woman who'd been with her for thirty years, chimed in. "I can see the blue of your eyes all the way over here. How striking."

Basking in the compliments, Wanda blew them kisses. "Is the gold lipstick too much?"

"Not on you." Tommie winked. "Gus will love it."

"For the dozenth time, there's nothing between us," Wanda insisted. She'd made the same statement yesterday. Why didn't people believe her?

The door opened. Polly entered followed by Gus. At the mere sight of the gorgeous male, Wanda's breath caught, and the feelings she'd denied moments ago rushed back. Who was she kidding? They'd been with her since the inspection on Monday.

Pretending she wasn't having heart palpitations, she smiled and headed to meet them. "Hello, Polly. Gus."

"Hey, Wanda." He looked her up and down, from the vee neckline of her black dress, past the thin, red belt at her waist, and down to her sheer, black hose and striped mules. "That's some outfit."

"Thanks."

While Polly fiddled with her cane and wasn't looking, he mouthed, "She knows about the Coffee Shack."

Great. It seemed the entire town had been briefed.

"This is her long appointment. I'll see you in an hour," he said.

Wanda nodded. "The color, cut and set should take about that long."

She watched him leave, keeping her expression neutral. But inside, her heart sighed with appreciation.

When she turned to Polly, a sly smile hovered on the older woman's lips. "At the drugstore yesterday, I ran into Betty Randall."

Words that had everyone staring at Wanda.

"I wouldn't believe everything I hear," she said, nice and loud. "There's nothing between Gus and me."

"He said the same thing." Polly's eyes twinkled, as if she didn't believe either of them.

This conversation was over. Wanda gestured toward the coffee pots. "How about a decaf?"

"Not today, thank you."

"All right then, let's get started." She offered her arm, and as usual, Polly ignored it.

Not quite sure how to broach the subject of getting together without sounding weird, Wanda edged into it. "How was your doctor's appointment?" she asked while waiting for Polly's hair color to set.

"It went well, thank you. I don't recall mentioning that I had an appointment."

"Oh. Maybe I imagined it."

"Gus must have told you."

"He may have. I don't remember."

Again with the knowing smile. Ignoring it, Wanda put on her happy face and jumped in with both feet. "Would you like to get together sometime?"

"You mean outside the salon?"

Polly looked so pleased, Wanda almost felt guilty for not thinking up the idea on her own. She nodded. "I'm thinking lunch."

"What a lovely idea. Why don't you come to my house? I rarely cook anymore, but I'll order from my favorite take-out. They make a low-sodium, low-fat pasta salad that's quite tasty."

Dying to see the house Polly refused to leave, Wanda quickly agreed. "I'd love to. What can I bring?"

"Just yourself. Which day works best for you?"

"Any Sunday or Monday."

"How about this Sunday? I usually have dinner with Gus and his dad, but I'm free for lunch. Unless you have church?"

"Not usually."

"Sunday it is."

10

Thursday dawned cool and rainy, and felt more like March than mid-April. Wearing a raincoat, Wanda knocked at the door of Gus's garage. She hadn't even rushed this morning. Not fussing with her hair, makeup or outfit du jour knocked an hour off the time she usually spent getting ready.

She hoped this was the right place. With no signage and the shades pulled on every window, she couldn't be sure.

Until Gus opened the door moments later. A decades-old Christopher Cross song spilled from the radio.

"You found me," he greeted.

"I wouldn't have without your directions. I don't see any signs posted. How do people know this is where you renovate cars?"

"Word of mouth and my website. I keep a lot of expensive equipment in here, and I don't want signs or anything that might draw attention to that. Fewer chances of break-ins that way. Come in."

"Even if I'm all wet?"

"The concrete floors won't mind. I'd offer to take

your coat, but..." He held up grease-stained hands. "Use the hook on the back of the door."

Even in a raggedy, stained oxford shirt with the sleeves cut off mid-biceps, loose, faded jeans, and sneakers, he was sexy. Which showed how far-gone she was.

She flipped her hood back, shrugged out of the dripping raincoat and hung it up. "It sure is wet out there," she pointed out in an effort to divert her wayward thoughts.

"It's been raining since before dawn." He nodded at her pony tail. "Cute. You could pass for seventeen."

She grimaced. "This is why I never wear my hair pulled back. I look so young."

"Only your face." His gaze traveled slowly over her loose jeans and old sweatshirt, and he made a sound of pure male appreciation. "Believe me, no one could mistake you for a teenage girl."

Her body started a slow sizzle, and she knew she was blushing. What in the world was she doing here? She made a show of checking her phone. "I have about an hour before I need to leave and get ready for work."

"Piece of cake. Home is only a ten-minute drive for you."

"And you?"

"About the same in the opposite direction. My place isn't far from the fire department."

"This doesn't look like a garage," she said, glancing around.

"The work space is in the rear of the building. I use this front area as my office. Let me wash up, then I'll show you around."

Rounding his battered but tidy desk, he moved to the large sink at the side of the room and lathered up. His biceps flexed against the cut-off sleeves. And his wrists.... Wanda let out a sigh of admiration, caught herself, and glanced away.

"Aunt Polly says you're having lunch this Sunday," he said over the hiss of the water.

"Did she mention the Coffee Shack, and that my reply matched yours? There is nothing between us." Except a healthy dose of animal magnetism easily ignored—if she was carved out of stone.

"Yep. It's good we told her the same thing."

Wanda nodded. "And that it's all behind us. I think you and your dad are sweet to have dinner with her on Sundays."

"We started that when we both moved out. She used to feed us at the house, but now we take her someplace quiet and get her home early."

"I feel sneaky and a little guilty about going over there with an agenda," Wanda said. "Why didn't I talk to her while I did her hair, instead of suggesting a get-together that she believes was all my idea?"

"Because the salon isn't the right time and place for what you have to say." Gus shut the water off and reached for a raggedy towel. "She needs to move, Wanda. You'll see for yourself when you get a look at the house. You're doing her, my dad and me a huge favor."

"That makes me feel better. I am looking forward to getting together."

"Then it's all good. I made fresh coffee." He gestured at the coffeemaker on the counter above a small refrigerator.

"How did you know?"

"Lucky guess." Mouth quirking, he filled a mug, then grabbed a carton of half-and-half from a small refrigerator.

After she fixed her drink, he nodded at the garage. "Come on, I'll show you around."

Wanda could hardly wait.

"THIS IS WHERE THE MAGIC HAPPENS," Gus said as he led Wanda through a doorway, into the brightly-lit space of his garage.

For a few seconds she didn't say anything, just looked around. He tried to see it through her eyes.

The big garage door that filled most of one wall. The tools arranged on pegboards, and the machines and equipment scattered around.

Her gaze lit on the Lincoln in the middle of the room. "Oh!" she said, and started toward it. "You never mentioned she's a convertible. And look at the colors —tan, with a dark brown top. Great color scheme."

Her awestruck tone turned him on. But lately, everything about her did. Don't go there, he chided himself. "At the moment, she isn't much to look at, but wait till you see the finished product."

"I disagree. With her classic lines, she's beautiful as is."

With that, Gus forgot they were supposed to be friends and nothing more. If this was the real Wanda, he was on board. Totally.

"Beautiful, all right," he murmured.

Her head swiveled his way, her eyes widening before her attention jerked to the Lincoln. Not before he saw the longing on her face.

Regardless what she said, she wanted him as bad as he wanted her.

Suddenly the garage felt ten degrees hotter. Or was it him?

She wandered toward the open hood and peered inside. "There's a lot of corrosion in here."

"You should have seen her when she first arrived." He showed her what he'd replaced so far.

She seemed interested, asking questions that revealed her substantial knowledge.

"You know more than you let on," he said, admiring her and liking her more by the minute.

"I must have absorbed more than I realized. Am I looking at the sparkplugs?"

He peered over her shoulder. "Yeah, and you can see that they're shot. By tomorrow, they'll be history."

Over the old oil odor permeating the engine, he caught a whiff of her lavender scent. God, he loved that smell. Fighting the urge to tug the band off her ponytail and bury his nose in her hair, he pointed out other parts that needed replacing. Stuff he was still searching for.

She leaned way in, and her very fine behind almost brushed his groin. Gus hardened painfully. He edged back.

Raising the single eyebrow that so intrigued him, Wanda glanced at him.

"It's that shampoo of yours," he said gruffly, turning her toward him. "Drives me wild."

The gold and green specks in her eyes darkened, reeling him in. Hardly aware of his actions, he wrapped his arms around her.

"Gus..." She sounded slightly breathless. "We shouldn't."

Beyond caring, he traced her soft bottom lip with his thumb. "We're two adults and we want this. Is that so wrong?"

"If we don't want to date each other, it is," she said, that perfect, pliable mouth driving him crazy.

"Who said anything about dating?"

"Okay, but we agreed not to kiss each other again."

He could barely form a thought, let alone argue. "Ask me to back off and I will. I don't think you want that."

She hesitated, trembled. "I don't." Rising on her toes, she pulled him down.

She tasted every bit as sweet as before. Better. Soft and warm and responsive, she pressed closer, as if trying to melt into him.

Gus groaned. "Let's sit down."

She gave a dazed nod, her cockeyed ponytail fluttering. Arousal tinted her skin pink, and her mouth looked slightly swollen. He'd never seen a more desirable woman.

Cupping her lush bottom, he lifted her. She wrapped her thighs around his waist. Aroused and pulsing, he carried to the work-table. In preparation for arranging car parts later, he'd laid out a clean towel. He set Wanda on it, kissed her eyelids and then returned to the mouth he couldn't get enough of.

Kissing her mouth again, he slid her forward. Tight against his erection, as physically close as a fully-dressed man and woman could be.

He ground into her, then had to stop before he embarrassed himself. Like an inexperienced kid with no self-control.

Eager to rock her world, he edged away from her cradling warmth and lifted her T-shirt.

He hadn't expected the orange sports bra, had figured her for the lacy lingerie type. She never failed to surprise him. "Nice bra."

"Believe me, if I'd ever guessed that you and I... You said to dress casual."

"I'm not sorry. You look sexy."

Wanda glanced down at the visible outlines of her nipples and flushed crimson. "I never noticed that."

"Hard to miss." Gus traced one nipple with his finger until the peak stiffened, and she stopped looking at herself.

Shivering, she let her head fell back. Loving her responsiveness, he teased the other nipple to the same rigid point.

"As much as I like you in this bra, it has to come off," he said. To his own ears, his voice sounded husky with need.

Heavy-lidded, she pulled it over her head.

Proud, pink areolae tipped her full-figured breasts. He swallowed. "You're even more perfect than I imagined."

"You've imagined me topless?"

"All the time." Awed by her beauty, he cupped her softness. Bent down and tasted each areola, licking and teasing until she was restless and moaning and gripping him with her thighs.

His body at full throttle, Gus unbuttoned her jeans.

He slid his fingers down the top of her panties. He was almost at his destination when she pushed him away. "No, Gus."

Aroused as he was, somehow he managed to stop. As soon as he retrieved her bra and shirt from the cement floor, she covered her breasts with them. Gus helped her to the floor.

"Where's the bathroom?" she asked.

He pointed at it. Moments later, she disappeared inside. In her absence, he calmed down enough to be coherent.

She came out, dressed, and moved toward him. With her ponytail straight and high on her head and her shirt smoothed over her hips, she looked exactly as she had when she'd walked in—except for the slight swelling of her thoroughly kissed mouth and the flush staining her face and neck.

His body jumped to life again, and it was all he could do not to reach for her. "You're something else, Wanda."

"Is that good or bad?" she asked, not quite meeting his eyes.

Her uncertainty tore at him. He needed to straighten out a few things, make sure they understood each other. "How about another cup of coffee?"

"No, thanks. I need to go and get ready for work."

Gus checked his watch. "We have a few minutes yet." He took her hand and led her to a bench near the tool boards. "Let's talk."

11

R ain pummeled the roof of the garage, competing with the Coke ad airing on the oldies station. The noise failed to drown out Wanda's thudding heart or silence her apprehension. Rehashing what had just happened was the last thing she wanted.

Why couldn't Gus leave it alone and let her go?

She was about to find out.

Nerves thrumming, she shifted on the hard bench and slid him a look. The seat they shared wasn't very big, not for a man of his size, and although they sat at opposite ends, she felt the warmth of his body.

"What's on your mind?" he said.

Wouldn't you know, the DJ played Billy Joel's "Honesty." The song and Gus's penetrating gaze prodded her to open up.

Admit how much she liked him? No, thanks. Foolishly blurting out her feelings wasn't her way. Not anymore.

The last time she'd taken the open and honest route, in a desperate effort to save her crumbling relationship with Wayne, he'd repaid her by stomping all over her heart.

I told you so. Always keep them guessing, Cindy had counseled in the aftermath. To this day, she continued to harp on the message.

Sound advice. Wanda bit her lip. "I don't have much to say."

"You sure about that?" Gus asked, all up in her face now.

She sensed he wouldn't quit until she gave him something. Resigned, she thunked her head against the wall. "I can't believe how I am with you. I'm not usually so...eager."

Bad enough she lacked the willpower to stop before they started. More upsetting was the powerful yearning for him that wouldn't quit. Her traitorous body still hummed and ached for more.

"We both got carried away. Again," he said. "It's the strong chemistry between us."

If only her feelings stopped at the physical level. She cared for him—way too much. Talk about a setup for future heartache. She knew this in her very soul, and yet she was strongly tempted to give in, forget the future, and enjoy the present.

Fighting that very bad idea and in desperate need of space, she stiffened her spine. "I really have to leave." She started to stand.

"I'm keeping an eye on the time," Gus said. "We still have four minutes to talk about us."

Us as in a *couple*? She sat again. "We both told your aunt Polly there is no us," she stated for the benefit of both Gus and her own wayward self.

"I'm with you there. But when we're alone together, you're tough to resist." Under his suddenly-lowered eyelids, his gaze smoldered. "I swore I wouldn't make a move on you this morning, but you've been so freaking amazing, I'd have to be dead not to react. Don't expect me to apologize for what happened."

His words caught her off-guard, puzzled her. "Define 'amazing.'"

"You're smart, beautiful and easy to talk to, and you get excited around classic cars. And you care about Aunt Polly." He grasped her hand, turned up her palm, and kissed the sensitive underside of her wrist, above her suddenly stuttering pulse. If she'd been on her feet, her knees would have wobbled.

God help her, she believed him. Then and there, she gave him another piece of her heart.

"To clarify, you're talking about this me," she said, extracting her hand and gesturing at herself. "The plain me right here."

"You couldn't be plain if you tried. I like this you."

He sounded as sincere as he had at the safety inspection, and she melted all over again.

Gorgeous Gus Viggio, a man who could have any woman on the planet, was attracted to her, even at her most drab, vanilla self. Less than a week ago, the possibility had seemed unimaginable.

Wanda wanted to hug him. She didn't. He now owned a chunk of her heart, and that scared her. Neither of them had much luck with relationships.

Cautious, she eyed him. "You'd better not be sweet-talking me to get into my panties."

"Oh, I definitely want sex with you, Wanda." Heat glimmered in his eyes.

She swallowed. "We can't, Gus."

"I know."

He didn't seem at all put off by her words. Flustered, she added, "Please don't ask to date me."

Although she'd entertained the idea herself earlier, she refused to give up the plan that had helped her get over Larry and saved her from jumping into anything new.

Besides, she was nowhere near to figuring out how to hold a man's interest. "I'm not ready."

"I want you anyway."

The potent words hung in the air, tempting and unsettling at the same time.

"You have to stop. So do I." Somehow. "I really do have to go," she said, rising again.

"I should get back to the Lincoln." He stood with her. "We ought to set up a time on Sunday to debrief, somewhere between your lunch with my aunt and my dinner."

Wanda nodded. "I'll call and fill you in."

"Or stop by here and tell me directly. I'll be working here all day Sunday."

Given her growing feelings, she didn't dare consider that. Avoiding face-to-face contact until she pulled herself together seemed best.

"Let's stick with a phone call," she said, silently congratulating herself for making the right choice. The safe choice, the one that would help her protect what was left of her heart.

AFTER WORK SATURDAY, Wanda, Nadia and Rochelle hopped in Rochelle's snazzy red Camaro and headed for Harvey's, the best pizza place in Guff's Lake. Even if it was located on the south side of town, a good thirty-minute drive from Tommie's, and Wanda's stomach was empty. The food was worth the time and wait.

After a long week and an insane day, she was tired enough to go home and veg. But she didn't want peace and quiet. She needed the noise and chaos of Harvey's —anything to drown out the antsy feeling that had been with her since she'd visited Gus's garage.

"We're a little overdressed for pizza," Nadia said. "Maybe we should go home, change, and meet here later."

"That'll take too long," Wanda said. "I'm too hungry and too tired to change."

Rochelle glanced at her through the darkness before she pulled out of her parking slot. "You do look super cute in that dress. My feet are killing me, but I'll survive. What a day, huh?"

Nadia groaned. "You can say that again. Could you believe Mrs. Pepple, making all that fuss over her daughter's black-tipped nails, calling them a symbol of witchcraft?" She snorted. "Marla's almost sixteen, and I gave her exactly what she wanted. She's not into witchcraft—she's just trying to draw attention to herself. She paid with her own money, and she seemed happy, so why make a big deal out of nothing?"

"It's probably a mother-daughter thing," Wanda said. "When I was fifteen, Cindy and I butted heads about everything."

"I doubt she yelled at the manicurist for painting your nails the way you wanted," Nadia said.

"Never."

Rochelle glanced at Nadia in the rearview mirror. "At least you didn't have to deal with Cassie Arst."

The young mother had tried to save money by coloring her hair at home. But something had gone wrong, changing her blonde hair to cotton-candy pink.

"You'd think she'd know that using peroxide to leach out the pink is a no-no." Rochelle shuddered.

"The strands were so brittle they almost broke in my hands."

"You handled the situation as well as any of us could have," Wanda pointed out.

"She wasn't satisfied. She blamed me for not making her look as good as before."

"Well, she left in a lot better shape than when she arrived. With all the crazies in the salon today, you'd think there was a full moon tonight."

Rochelle blew out a loud breath. "After our stressful day, we need alcohol. Shall we share a pitcher or a bottle of wine?"

"I vote for beer," Wanda said. "And an extra-large pizza with the works. Remember, if we eat on the premises—"

"The calories don't count," the three of them chimed in unison. They broke into much-needed laughter.

The calorie comment led to grumblings about the chocolates that always floated around the salon. None of them could resist, and Wanda had given up battling the extra five pounds on her hips.

At last, Rochelle turned into the parking area at Harvey's.

"Look at all these cars," Nadia lamented. "We'll never get a table."

"Of course, we will," Wanda assured her. "Half the people here are picking up takeout orders."

After creeping around, looking for a place to park, Rochelle finally found a space between a truck and a navy Jeep Cherokee that looked a lot like Gus's car. In the dim parking lot lights, Wanda couldn't be sure. Needing to find out, she exited the Camaro and went straight to the Jeep's license plate. The Professional

Firefighter tag gave her the answer. This Cherokee belonged to Gus.

He's here.

A thrill rushed through her, followed by panic. Still dealing with a bad case of lust caused by the delicious kisses and more they'd shared, she wasn't up for facing him tonight.

"On second thought, Harvey's is way more crowded than I thought." She nodded at the big picture window, through which the crowd inside was visible. "We could be waiting forever. Maybe we should go someplace else."

Her friends gave her startled looks. "But I have my choppers set for pizza," Nadia said. She squinted at the license plate before her eyes widened. "Ah...this is Gus's car."

Wanda nodded.

"If it were me and I'd kissed him at the Coffee Shack, I'd welcome running into him tonight. Are you positive you don't want to get back in the game and go out with him?"

Wanda shook her head. "At the moment, I don't even want to see the man. I'm trying to stick to my plan."

Rochelle let out a resigned breath. "We drove all the way out here for pizza, but if you're that set on not running into Gus, let's go someplace else."

Grateful her best friends understood, Wanda relaxed. "I'll make it up to you, I swear."

On the heels of her words, the front door opened. Wouldn't you know, Gus stepped outside, along with two other big, good-looking males.

Bright perimeter lights around the building illuminated their broad shoulders and clean-cut, rugged faces—faces Wanda recognized from the same calendar that profiled Gus. One of the men cradled enough large pizza boxes to feed a small army.

Gus was the tallest of the three and her attention gravitated to him. He said something that made his companions laugh, and an irresistible grin filled his face.

She knew exactly when he spotted her. The light-heartedness faded into a focused, more intent expression.

Even from a distance, his gaze hooked her. She couldn't glance away if she tried. Her body heaved a yearning sigh and her nipples hardened.

"Speak of the devil," Rochelle murmured in her ear. "And get a load of the gorgeous men with him. They look familiar, but I can't place them."

"They're in the fire department benefit calendar, too," Wanda explained, without taking her eyes off Gus.

"Anybody have a fan? Cause I'm kinda hot," Nadia murmured as the men started forward. "And we're about to meet them."

12

After several days' time and space, Gus came to his senses. He realized getting together with Wanda was a bad idea. Even if he did like the woman he'd glimpsed at the garage, she didn't need a guy with his lousy track record in her life. He didn't want to get involved, either. It just wouldn't work. His thoughts went no further than that—if you didn't count spending every waking hour and a fair bit of dreamtime lusting after her.

Bound and determined to put all that behind him, he hadn't figured on running into her tonight. Let alone seeing her in *do me* heels and a short, tight dress that fit her curves like a glove.

Not even a hint of the Wanda from the garage—the real Wanda. All the same, he forgot about steering clear.

Owen jerked his chin over the four jumbo pizza boxes in his hands. "Check out those three fine ladies standing by your Jeep, checking us out."

"Oh, I am," Max murmured.

"I know them," Gus said. "They work at Tommie's Hair and Nails. Wanda is the one in red."

"So that's the woman we've been hearing about."

Max whistled under his breath. "No wonder you like her."

"She's a looker, all right," Owen added. "Great body. With that spiky hair, she could pass for a rocker chick."

They weren't the only men gawking at Wanda and her attractive lady friends. A group on their way inside slowed and stared with undisguised interest. Gus didn't realize he'd let out a warning growl until Owen eyed him.

"Easy, big buddy. Guys are checking her out, but she's not looking back. Gonna introduce us?"

Gus had already started forward. He stopped in front of Wanda. Not near enough to put his hands on her but close enough to catch a whiff of her lavender scent. Tonight her hair was black with bright red streaks tipping the spiky parts.

"Hi, Gus." She didn't quite smile.

Neither did he. "Didn't expect to see you tonight."

"We're huge fans of Harvey's pizza." She gestured toward her friends. "You know Rochelle and Nadia from the salon."

Gus nodded hello, then introduced his buds. "Meet Owen and Max, two of my crewmates."

Wanda's companions looked awestruck. Gus chalked that up to the calendar and the height he and his buds had over them.

Rochelle, the tallest of the women, with normal, chin-length hair, nodded Owen's way. "You have a lot of pizza there."

Owen gave her a cocky grin. "We played football this afternoon. We're hungry."

"You and Max played softball," Gus corrected. "I worked on the Lincoln all day."

"Yeah, but you were so wrapped up in that car you forgot to eat lunch," Owen reminded him.

"Where did you play?" Nadia asked Max. Olive-skinned, with a thick braid down her back, she stood taller than Wanda but shorter than Rochelle.

"At the field near Guff's Lake. We play firefighters from other shifts."

While Max and Owen launched into stories about the game, Gus caught Wanda sneaking looks at him, longing glances a guy would have to be dead to ignore. At first, she jerked her attention away, but before long, they started speaking silently through their eyes. Stuff too hot and private to share.

Gus wanted her bad. She wanted him, too, just as she had in the garage. Nothing in the world more powerful than that.

He fought his desire, ordered himself to cool it, and attempted to participate in the chit-chat. Distracting himself proved impossible. Soon, he gave up any pretense of following the verbal conversation.

"Why don't we get out of here and go someplace?" he said in a voice too low for anyone but Wanda to hear.

"I thought you were starving," she replied in an equally low voice.

"I am." He let his eyes do the talking on that one.

She glanced away, bit her lip. "I meant what I said at the garage. We can't."

At least one of them was thinking straight. He nodded. "Good luck tomorrow."

For a moment she stared at him blankly, as if she had no idea what he meant. Then she seemed to remember. "You mean Polly. I'm a little nervous. I haven't figured out exactly what to say."

"Be yourself and you'll come out okay."

"Because that works so well for you."

"You're not her nagging nephew. She really likes you."

"Now, but after I talk to her..." Wanda's hands twisted together at her waist. "I don't want to lose her friendship over this."

"If it bothers you that much, don't do it."

"You'd let me off the hook?"

Gus sure as hell hoped she didn't back out, but he wasn't about to twist her arm. "There is no hook," he said. "Do what feels right for you."

She stopped fidgeting, thought about that, and frowned. "If something happened to her because I didn't step up, I couldn't live with myself. Someone needs to talk sense into her. It may as well be me. Even if I fail."

Her determination made him want her more than ever. Deterred by the reckless thought, he stepped back. "I appreciate that. Have a good night, and keep me posted."

Soon, his buds indicated they were ready to split. "Nice chatting with you ladies," Gus said. "Our pizzas are getting cold, and there's a PGA tournament recap to watch. See you all later."

CUTLERY CLATTERED, glasses clinked and conversation buzzed through Harvey's Pizza. Not an empty booth in sight, but Wanda, Rochelle and Nadia found a table near the kitchen. The harried waitstaff bustled non-stop through the swinging door, emerging with mouthwatering arrays of pizzas.

"I'm so glad you changed your mind about eating

here," Rochelle said, licking her lips as she studied the menu.

"Only because we ran into Gus and his friends outside." Nadia sighed. "They're just as hot as he is. With those looks, they could be stuck-up jerks. Yet they seem like decent guys."

Wanda agreed, although in her opinion, Owen and Max couldn't compare with Gus. "Owen likes you, I think," she told Rochelle. "And Max certainly seemed interested in Nadia."

"Not interested enough to ask for our numbers," Rochelle said. "But that's okay. I have my eye on someone else."

"Oh? Who might that be?"

"His name is Matt Wolfe. He walked in needing a trim yesterday, and I cut his hair. Great hair. He has the biggest brown eyes. When I finished, he asked me out."

"Where were we when this happened?" Wanda asked.

"In the back, taking your lunch break."

"And you didn't see fit to mention this important fact to your two best friends?"

"When did we have time to talk? Anyway, Matt and I going out dancing at Lucky Joe's tomorrow night." The local bar and restaurant offered live music every weekend, including Sundays. "I'll let you know how it goes."

"You'd better," Nadia said.

Rochelle eyed Wanda. "The way you and Gus made eyes at each other tonight... If that's a break from men, I'm the Easter Bunny."

"You noticed, huh?" Ready to discuss her confusion, Wanda gestured both women closer. "Swear you won't tell anyone what I'm about to share."

Nadia mimed locking her lips and Rochelle crossed her heart.

The waitress chose that moment to arrive at their table. After taking their orders, she left. All ears, Wanda's friends canted toward her with inquiring expressions.

She started at the beginning. "I never really mentioned what happened that morning at the Coffee Shack. My day started with a wake-up call from Tommie. She asked me to open the salon right away. I scrambled to shower and dress and get over there. I managed to fix my hair at the salon, but didn't have time to put on my full face before I left to meet Gus. I hate to be seen in public without makeup."

"What woman doesn't?" Nadia agreed.

"I decided to run with it and be deliberately boring. That way, I wouldn't encourage Gus."

Rochelle nodded. "Because of your plan."

"Right. I didn't flirt, make constant conversation or crack jokes. We talked like platonic friends."

"After what I just witnessed, I'm having trouble believing that," Rochelle said.

Although Gus hadn't laid a finger on Wanda tonight, certain parts of her vibrated as if he had. "That day, I may have underestimated the chemistry between us," she admitted. She lowered her voice. "But while we were sitting and chatting and sipping coffee, I had no idea Gus would kiss me later." Granted, all her synapses had fired definite sizzle alerts. "I don't think he planned it, either. When we ducked out of sight to avoid Betty, it just happened."

"You expect us to believe that?" Rochelle asked.

Wanda glared at her. "Do you want to hear this or not?" She went on, "I told myself it was just a kiss, that as long we weren't dating, I hadn't veered from my plan."

The waitress delivered a pitcher of beer and the pizza, and for a while, conversation ground to a halt. Then Nadia reminded her. "You were saying?"

"I intended to forget all about those kisses," Wanda went on. "But that hasn't worked so well. All Gus has to do is look at me and I want more." She buried her face in her hands and groaned.

"You're only human," Nadia said. "That man would tempt a saint."

"I don't want to be tempted, and I assured myself it wouldn't happen again. Then the other day at his garage—"

"Garage?" Nadia echoed.

"He knows I like classic cars. He invited me to take a look at the Lincoln he's restoring."

"When exactly was that?" Rochelle asked.

"Earlier this week."

Rochelle's jaw dropped. "And you get on my case for not mentioning Matt sooner?"

"As you said, we haven't time to talk. I wish you could see that car. She's a convertible, and what a stunner she—"

Nadia made an impatient sound. "Could you get back to you and Gus?"

"We sort of got into a kissing thing there, too."

"Sort of?"

Wanda recalled everything that had happened and felt herself blush. "You know what I mean."

"No, but I'd like to."

"Details, please," Rochelle seconded.

Not about to supply any, Wanda cut to the chase. "Let's just say, we got a little hot and heavy."

Nadia lifted her eyebrows in a wowza and Rochelle smiled like the Cheshire cat.

"We didn't have sex," Wanda assured them. "I'm not that weak." Barely. "He thinks it's cool I'm into classical cars and he likes me in loose, old clothes and less makeup. And we all know that without my cute outfits and makeup, I'm not much to look at."

Rochelle rolled her eyes. "Baloney. You're adorable, no matter what."

Nadia added a fond smile. "What she said."

"You only say that because you're my BFFs. If you saw me first thing in the morning, you'd change your minds."

"No one looks good straight out of bed," Rochelle said. "The point is, whether or not you dress nice and wear makeup, Gus is interested in you."

"And that scares me to death."

Comprehension dawned on Rochelle's face. "You're falling for him."

Wanda gave a miserable nod. "I'm trying not to, but you know me."

"If a guy treats you halfway decently, you're a goner. Then you get hurt."

Bingo.

"Maybe Gus is different," Nadia said. "From the way he looked at you tonight, I'd guess he's falling for you, too. Would a trial relationship be so wrong?"

"That wouldn't be wise. His luck with women is about as bad as mine with men. Getting involved could turn out to be a huge mistake."

During the beat of glum silence that followed, Rochelle reached for the pitcher. "What are you going to do?"

"Pretend he doesn't rock my world and hope he goes away."

13

Lunching at Polly's sunlit kitchen table, Wanda understood why she loved her home—even if it was way too big for an elderly woman with mobility issues.

This room oozed warmth and hominess. Three shelves of well-used cookbooks testified to Polly's former cooking skills. A ceramic rooster sitting on the tile counter added extra color to the pencil-thin red stripes on cream wallpaper, and a clock shaped like the sun had to be vintage 1960s.

Who cared if the appliances and overhead light were outdated? The high ceilings and roominess more than compensated for any defects. A person could breathe here and invite friends over for private conversations.

As a child, Wanda had dreamed of living in a house similar to this one. She still did—if and when she found the right man to share it with.

"A penny for your thoughts," Polly said.

"I was thinking about what a great kitchen this is." And that it no longer suited Polly's needs.

"I've had some good times here." With more than half her pasta salad remaining on her plate, Polly pushed it aside. "Lots of wonderful memories from when my husband, Martin, was alive."

Wearing a nostalgic smile, she stared into space, at something only she could see. Not wanting to interrupt what appeared to be a fond look back, Wanda sat quietly.

Before long, Polly spoke again. "For a while after my husband passed, I got pretty lonely in this big old house. I even thought about selling. But this was my dream home. Martin poured his heart and soul into it, and leaving didn't seem right. I felt terrible for even entertaining the thought. When Gus and his dad moved in, I was doubly glad I stayed."

If that wasn't the perfect opening for a conversation about downsizing. But Wanda wanted to hear Polly's memories. "Gus mentioned how lucky he was that you raised him."

"Did he? How sweet." Polly's eyes misted. "When he moved in, he was seven years old, and such a little tyke. A string bean with arms like toothpicks. A person would never have guessed he would grow into the robust man he is today. If you're interested, I have photos on the mantel."

"I would love to see them."

"All right, let's go look."

Resisting the urge to help Polly stand, Wanda brushed crumbs from her sandwich into her hand and emptied them onto her plate.

In the living room, where the furniture looked high-quality but faded, Aunt Polly led her to the hearth. The painted white brick fireplace provided a nice contrast with the dark wood of the mantel. Wanda loved the wood floors, the oriental rug and the natural beams across another high ceiling.

"What a beautiful room," Wanda said.

"Isn't it?" Polly pointed out various photos on the mantel. "This is Gus's first grade school picture, taken before his parents separated."

The photographer had caught the adorable boy at the tail-end of laughter—eyes crinkling with mirth, his mouth slightly open, revealing gaps from where he'd lost his two front teeth. Already, he wore the same killer smile that charmed her now. "I recognize that impish expression."

"Today that's his teasing grin," Polly said. "When he was a child, it meant he was up to something I disapproved of. Skipping school to see a matinee with his friends, climbing dangerous rocks, wasting his allowance on junk food..." Wearing a fond smile, she shook her head. "That boy was a handful."

Laughing, Wanda turned to a photo of a big man in a firefighter uniform, grinning up at a young Gus seated proudly at the wheel of a fire engine. "That must be Gus's father."

"Edmondo, or Ed for short." Polly nodded at the black-and-white photo. "This is Martin and me, before we left for our honeymoon."

The couple looked radiant, a young, beautiful Polly beaming into her older husband's loving face. Wanda envied them. Would she ever experience that kind of love?

Another photo showed them embracing in a passionate kiss.

"We'd been married about a year here," Polly said. "I can't believe I was ever that young." She turned away. "I'm going to sit down in my Barcalounger. It's easy for me to get out of. If you like rocking chairs, the one in the corner used to be my favorite."

Wary of tiring her, Wanda hesitated. "Maybe I

should go." She should have broached the subject of moving when she had the chance.

"Stay awhile longer. I'm enjoying our visit. Pull that rocking chair over here."

Wanda did as she was told and sat down. "Tell me more about when Gus and his dad moved in."

Polly looked thoughtful. "Belinda had left unexpectedly. Ed was crushed, and you can imagine Gus's confusion."

Remembering Gus's comments on the subject, Wanda nodded.

"My heart ached for them both," Polly said. "At the time, I was fifty-four. You wouldn't know it by looking at me now, but I had plenty of pep. I made a vow to mother Gus as if he were my own."

Wanda nodded. "He mentioned that you stepped down from your job as head librarian to work part-time."

"He did, did he?" Polly gave her a speculative look.

"The adjustments you made can't have been easy."

"We had our challenges, but I'm proud of the man Gus has become." Polly yawned. "I hate to shoo you out, Wanda, but I need to clean up the lunch mess and rest before Gus and Ed pick me up for dinner."

It was time to bring up moving. "Will you let me clean up before I go?" Wanda offered.

"That would be lovely."

Polly returned to her seat at the kitchen table. Wanda took care of the dishes, put the leftovers away and began with a question. "With Gus and his father living in their own places... Does this house ever feel like too much?"

"Sometimes, but as I explained, I could never sell."

"I get that. The thing is, your husband designed this home for the younger you. A lot has happened since then. You've changed, but the house has stayed the same. It doesn't seem to fit your lifestyle anymore."

"And you think I should move into one of those retirement communities? I know what happens in those places. Well, not to this woman." Polly raised her head high. "I have always been independent, and I intend to stay that way."

"You would be," Wanda said. "Several of my clients live in retirement communities. Their lives haven't changed much, except they no longer have to worry about taking care of their homes and yards anymore."

"Have you ever visited a retirement community?"

"No, but—"

"Gus put you up to this, didn't he?" Polly fisted her hands on her hips. "I've told him countless times I don't want to move. I won't! I suppose I'll have to set him straight again at dinner tonight. You be sure and tell him, too."

She looked so cross, Wanda winced. She hated to upset anyone, especially a woman she considered a friend. "Don't be angry with me, Polly. I just want you to be safe and happy."

"I am safe and except for the past few minutes, happy. In the future, unless I ask for your help, stay out of my private business."

Wanda promised she would and apologized, but Polly remained hostile. Moments later, she returned to her Barcalounger.

Regretting she'd ever said a word about moving, Wanda let herself out.

~

GUS CHECKED THE CLOCK, surprised that it was after four. He'd lost track of the time, but when working on a classic car he often did. By now, he should have heard from Wanda. Her silence could mean anything.

Antsy for a report, he washed up at the sink. He needed to get home, pronto, and shower before he picked up his father and Aunt Polly.

He needed an update from Wanda. If she didn't contact him soon, he'd phone her.

As he shut the water off, his cell phone rang. Wanda. About time. After wiping his hands on his jeans, he answered. "I was beginning to wonder. How did lunch go?"

"Great until I mentioned moving. Polly figured out fast that you put me up to it."

"She did, huh? Was she receptive?"

"Heck, no. I got the same response you always get. She's not moving. She bit my head off for butting in. I apologized and promised not to anymore—for all the good that did. She's mad at me, and I don't like it."

Having been there more than a few times, Gus understood. "At least you tried. She'll get over it."

"She'd better. Polly is one of my favorite clients, and I don't want to lose her business or her friendship."

"You're her favorite stylist, and she looks forward to your weekly appointments. She won't replace you." He fished his keys from his pocket.

"What makes you so sure?"

Gus wasn't, but he couldn't imagine Aunt Polly switching. "I'll talk to her."

"Please don't. I'd rather forget it ever happened and for things to be normal between us. Ha. She did make some interesting comments, though."

"Such as?" he asked, locking the door to the garage and heading into the gray afternoon.

"That she'd feel 'wrong' selling the house her husband custom-designed for her. Also, she worries about losing her independence if she moves."

"Only if she can no longer care for herself." Gus hoped that path lay in the distant future.

"Still, that's what she believes. She must know someone who had a bad experience at a retirement community."

"As a matter of fact, her best friend had just moved into an apartment at one of those places when she fell and broke her hip. She got too frail to leave her bed, and she never did heal. A few months later, she passed away. That has to be why Aunt Polly refuses to set foot in a retirement community. I never put the two to-gether, but you did."

Bowled over by Wanda's insight, he unlocked the car and slid into the driver's seat.

"What happened to Polly's friend has nothing to do with her own situation," Wanda said. "If she'd meet some of the healthy people who live in retirement communities, she might change her mind."

"Too damn stubborn. She's never been flexible." Understatement of the year.

"Now she's mad at us both. I knew I shouldn't get involved. You owe me big-time, Gus."

Feeling lousy about the whole situation, he sat in the car and scrubbed his hand over his face. "I'd treat you to dinner someplace, but that's not a good idea. Not only because you're on a break. What you said at the garage...You're right, I have to stop wanting you."

"I wish you'd tell me how to do that," she said, sounding as desperate as he was.

"Keep busy, stay active, stuff like that." Same things he'd done all along. None of it dampened his hunger for Wanda, but he wouldn't let that discourage him.

She mumbled something about eating more

chocolate, and then blew out a heavy breath. "We should also avoid being alone together."

"Yeah. How do I make it up to you about Aunt Polly?"

"I don't want anything, except a promise you'll never again ask me to talk to her about her private business."

"You have my word." He switched to Bluetooth and headed out.

"The visit wasn't all bad," Wanda said. "She showed me a photo of you and your dad from his fire-fighting days. Is that why you joined the Guff's Lake Fire Department, to be like him?"

"Pretty much. We're a lot alike." Especially when it came to women and relationships.

"He must be pleased. I also saw some cute photos of you when you were little. My favorite is your first-grade picture, where you don't have any front teeth."

Although Wanda couldn't see Gus, shook his head at the Jeep's ceiling. "Those old pictures have been on her mantelpiece way too long."

"She loves you, Gus, and she's very proud of you."

"I know."

"What a wonderful house," Wanda went on. "And all the memories... I understand why she's so attached."

"I can't argue with that. With the big yard and kids all up and down the block, it was a great place to grow up."

"There are still kids in the neighborhood. I saw a bunch of them playing outside."

"That house needs work and a family to take care of it, but I won't hold my breath. I'll be in touch."

Aunt Polly was quiet while Gus helped her into the Jeep. From the backseat, his dad greeted her. As soon as she buckled herself in, Gus shut the passenger door and rounded the car to the driver's seat.

He hadn't even pulled out of her driveway before she started in.

"You have some nerve, asking Wanda to talk to me about moving."

In the rearview mirror, Gus and his dad shared a Here we go look.

"That came from a place of love for you," his father explained.

Turning her head toward him, Aunt Polly frowned. "You were in on this, too?"

"No, but I approve. We're worried about your welfare. We want you to be safe and taken care of. From everything I've heard about Wanda, she shares our concerns."

"So Gus has mentioned her to you." A smile replaced Aunt Polly's frown. "What did he tell you?"

"That you got mad when she tried to talk to you," Gus said. "She's upset."

The frown returned. "Filled you in, did she? I can't believe the two of you went behind my back, talking about what's best for me, as if I was too feeble-minded to think for myself. I'm so angry I might cancel my Wednesday hair appointment."

Wanda worried about that very thing. "Don't blame her," Gus said. "She didn't even want to do it."

"Then she shouldn't have. I wish you would all stop carping at me." Aunt Polly crossed her arms, set her jaw, and stared out the passenger window.

Gus bit back a few choice words. He wasn't about to apologize, when the fault lay with her own stubbornness.

No one spoke again until they were a block from The Rogue, a Denny's-like restaurant Aunt Polly enjoyed.

She finally angled her head at him. "There is a way for both you and Wanda to get back in my good graces."

Gus eyed her. "What's that?"

"Go on a date."

No effing way. Their attraction to each other was too damn dangerous. "You don't get to dictate who I date," he growled.

"Fine. I'll cancel the appointment."

"You wouldn't."

"Oh, no? Try me."

He swore under his breath. "She'll turn me down."

"Why would she do that?" his father asked.

Not about to get into the ins and outs of the situation, Gus shrugged. "She's been hurt, and she's taking a rest from dating."

So was he.

"Pish posh." Aunt Polly dismissed the words with an airy wave of the hand. "Anyone with eyes can see what a handsome man you are, Gus. You've had plenty of girlfriends, and you know how to woo a woman. Figure out something Wanda wants and offer it to her. Suggest a place she'd like to go." Without pausing, she dropped a new threat. "If she refuses you, then I just might find a new hairdresser at a different salon. The only way I'll forgive her is if she agrees to a date with you."

"That's not fair." He gave her a black look, which she ignored. She knew she'd pinned him to the mat.

Want to or not, he needed to ask Wanda out, and she needed to go.

Hell.

~

WANDA CONSIDERED HERSELF A METICULOUS HOUSEKEEPER—THANKS to Cindy, who'd schooled her from an early age. She kept her apartment reasonably tidy at all times and set aside time on Sunday for a thorough cleaning. Having spent several hours at Polly's house, she didn't finish the usual housework until early evening. She stuck a frozen potpie into the oven, then started another load of laundry.

After eating, she went to work on herself, beginning with a deep-cleansing facial mud mask. While she waited for the mask to dry, she selected a new hair color for the week. Dark toffee. She was sorting through her vast supply of possibilities for contrasting streaks when the security buzzer downstairs beeped.

Who could that be? Rochelle was out dancing with Matt, and Nadia had gone to the movies with a friend. Wanda wasn't expecting anyone.

Frowning, she pressed the intercom in her kitchen. "Hello?"

"Hey, it's Gus," he boomed in the deep voice that curled her toes.

Gus, downstairs? And her with mud on her face, dressed in threadbare sweats, and a do-rag covering her hair. Not even Nadia and Rochelle had seen her look this bad.

Panicky, she stalled for time. "What are you doing here?"

"Invite me up and I'll tell you."

Aside from looking like crap, being alone with him was dangerous. She hesitated.

"It's about Aunt Polly," Gus said. "I just came from dinner with her."

The breath whooshed from her lungs. "Tell me she's okay."

"She's too scrappy to be anything but. Let me in."

Yes or no? She waged a brief, silent battle as the need to keep her heart safe duked it out with her burning curiosity. In the end, the need to know won.

"All right, but I'm kind of busy. You can't stay long," she said to mollify the warnings firing in her brain. "Give me five minutes."

The second she buzzed the downstairs security door open, she raced for the bathroom and scrubbed the mud from her face. She looked squeaky-clean and pale, but there was nothing she could do about that. She hurried to the bedroom to change. Problem was, her most flattering jeans were going through the rinse cycle and her favorite shirt was dripping dry.

She was contemplating changing into a dress, when common sense hit. Why bother? Gus had never seen her at her absolute worst. Once he did, he might not want her anymore, solving her problems in one easy swoop. Not that the strategy had worked before, but she hadn't looked this awful. She half wished she'd left the mud on her face.

She answered the door in bare feet, revealing the badly chipped toenail polish she intended to repair after she colored her hair.

"Hey," he said, his gaze taking in the do-rag, sweats and her nasty-looking toes. "Are you wearing that orange sports bra under your T-shirt?"

Yes, and darned if her nipples didn't harden. She crossed her arms. "This is my cleaning day."

"On a Sunday night?"

"I got a late start."

He glanced at the lopsided, purple vase on her bookshelf. "Interesting piece. Modern art?"

"It's supposed to be a vase. I made it. I know it's ugly, but I'm proud of it."

"Cool. Did you take one of Jillian Metzger's classes?"

"Several. How did you guess?"

"I've seen her studio. She's involved with Rafe Donato, one of my crewmates."

"I knew that." And envied the woman for finding true love.

His gaze strayed past her to the sliding glass door off the living room. "So, that's the balcony you talked about."

Wanda nodded. To her relief, he didn't ask to sit out there, which would be way too romantic. But then, like her, he was trying to move on.

She gestured him toward an armchair before sitting on the loveseat across from the coffee table. "Is Polly still angry with me?"

His expression grew solemn. "And me. We're in the subbasement of the doghouse. She offered us a way out, though. That's why I'm here."

"What does she want, a month of free haircuts?"

"If only it was that easy. She expects us to go on a date."

Wanda's jaw dropped. "She knows my feelings on that."

"I reminded her about your break from dating, but she ignored me. She mentioned twice that forgiving either of us hinges on our going out together."

"That's blackmail!"

"Tell me about it. She's made up her mind." Gus spread his hands in a helpless gesture.

"In other words, we're stuck. Lovely." Wanda wasn't sure what to do. "I need time to think about this. I'll get back to you later."

"There is one more thing, something you won't like any better," he said.

What else could there possibly be?

"She threatened to cancel the Wednesday appointment. She said she might even find a different salon."

Wanda groaned. "Would she really do that?"

"Who can say? She sounded like she meant business."

"I don't like this at all." Frowning, she studied the small hole on the cuff of her sleeve. "I don't usually go out during the week, but if I did, I don't see how it could possibly happen before Polly's Wednesday appointment. Your forty-eight hour shift starts tomorrow, and that's my only other day off this week." Her mind spun. "If you and I went out, and I'm not saying we will, it'd have to be after Wednesday. Which means Polly's going to cancel and I may never see her again. Now I'm mad at her."

"It sucks, that's for sure. As long as we set a date to go out in the near future, she'll keep the appointment and forget about leaving Tommie's."

"She drives one heck of a tough bargain. How do you feel about this, Gus?"

"I'm pissed as hell, but she didn't leave us much choice. As long as you and I are on the same page about what we want and don't want out of this, we should come through okay."

"How do we know if we're on the same page?" she asked. "Aside from our mutual decision to stop wanting each other."

His gaze darted over her, flashing hunger and heat. She trembled with longing.

Nope, that wasn't working so well.

"If we're going to do this, we should set some ground rules," she said. To help keep her wayward desire in check.

"Such as?"

"We said we weren't going to be alone together," she reminded him.

"No problem. We'll be in a public place."

"Good. And no touching or kissing."

"Agreed. How about Wednesday night?"

"I have a seven-thirty consult with a bride-to-be about doing her hair for her wedding. That could take awhile."

"You work late Thursdays and Fridays. We could go after you get off one of those evenings, or Saturday night."

"Let's make it Thursday, but only because Polly's twisting my arm. You can tell her I said so."

15

Thanks to a slow Monday at the fire department, the captain cleared Gus to spend the afternoon doing safety inspections.

When he returned to the station late that afternoon, he headed for the gym upstairs, along with Owen and a couple other crewmates. Workouts helped them all stay in shape.

"You're in a much better mood than the other day," Owen commented after a grueling cardio kickboxing session that left them all dripping in sweat. "Must be the exercise. Have you talked to Wanda?"

That caught Gus off-guard. "Why would you ask?"

"The way you two looked at each other Saturday night, I figured you'd call her."

"Her infamous plan crumbles under your charm," Rafe quipped.

"Not exactly. I asked her to talk to Aunt Polly about moving. That backfired, and Aunt Polly's mad at both of us. She claims she won't forgive us unless Wanda and I go out. Wanda calls it a blackmail date."

"Polly did that?" Owens's jaw dropped in disbelief. "Remind me to never get on her bad side."

"A date is a date," Rafe commented. "Where are you taking her?"

"We haven't decided."

Owen slanted him a look. "You say she's been jerked around quite a bit. You don't want to be the next guy to pull her chain."

True. Luckily, neither of them wanted to get involved. They'd also set down rules to keep their strong physical connection under wraps.

"There isn't a chance in hell of that happening," he said. He was sure of it.

MONDAY EVENING, Wanda stood in front of her closet and studied her clothes with a critical eye. Which outfits looked best with dark toffee hair and the platinum she'd painted on in sections? While she debated between a flattering cream dress with dark brown accents and a clingy teal-colored top and lacy black skirt, her cell phone chirped.

Gus. Her stomach fluttered way too much, and for all of two rings, she debated whether to answer. Unable to stop herself, she picked up. "Things must be slow at the station tonight," she said by way of a greeting.

"It's been that way, but you never know what the night will bring. How was your day?"

She gave him brownie points for bothering to ask. "Not bad. The client who's getting married rescheduled to this afternoon. She asked me to do her hair and all six of her bridesmaids."

"In other words, you didn't get the day off."

"No, but I slept in this morning, which was nice. The money I'll make from the wedding will go a long way toward what I need for the down payment on the bank loan."

"That's good news. About our date Thursday...let's have dinner."

"I'm here until nine. I'll never hold out that long." For that reason, she'd purchased a rotisserie-cooked chicken for dinner Thursday and Friday nights.

"Then eat twice. I will."

She laughed at that. "I'll stick to one meal, thanks. A nightcap and dessert sounds better. Where shall we go?"

"Your choice. Tell me what you want."

His low, intimate tone reverberated through her, making her long for things that would only end up hurting her. Love. Specifically, Gus's love. Yes, her heart whispered.

As usual, the dang thing was way ahead of itself. This time, thanks to her rock-solid plan, Wanda refused to let it rule. Especially when she had no idea what he cared about other than sex.

"I'll tell you what I don't want. A romantic evening," she said.

"I hear ya. That's what those rules are for. We could to go Marv's. Nothing romantic there, and the restaurant offers a decent selection of pies and outstanding fries and burgers. In case you're hungry for more substantial food."

Wanda was quite familiar with the place. Before she and Larry had broken up, the blue-collar beer and hamburger joint on the south side of town had been one of her favorite places to unwind.

But since then? "I don't know," she said.

"Can you think of any other place in town that serves dessert and stays open past ten?"

He had a point.

"We could switch to Saturday night, when you're off at six," he suggested. "More options then."

"Saturday night seems too much like an actual date."

"Saturday night is out. Got it. What's wrong with Marv's?"

Wanda saw no reason to lie. "That's where I met Larry."

"You're thinking you'll run into him." His clipped tone spoke volumes as to what he thought about that.

"I might. Marv's is his go-to place. But I enjoy going there, and I'm tired of staying away to avoid seeing him. Who cares if I do? I'm so over that man."

"You certain of that?"

The cheating and lies, the money he'd borrowed and still owed her, his total self-absorption? "Absolutely," she replied without hesitation. It'd be good to show him how well she was doing without him. "I'd love to go to Marv's."

"We have a place. All right! What time should I pick you up?"

"Let's meet at the salon at nine. At the end of the evening, you can drop me back there and I'll drive myself home." Making the evening feel even less like a date.

"Fine by me. See you then."

16

When Gus brought Polly in for her trim Wednesday, her gloating smile irritated the heck out of Wanda.

Gus frowned at his aunt and shook his head at the ceiling. "Forty-five minutes good?" he asked Wanda.

Having no interest in spending one extra minute with the woman, Wanda had booked an appointment directly following this one. "Thirty is better," she said.

He nodded, then left.

Dispensing with niceties, Wanda gestured toward the station. "Let's go, Polly."

The scheming blackmailer seemed not to notice. "I'm thrilled you and Gus have a date tomorrow night," she cooed as they made their way toward Wanda's station.

Enough was enough. Wanda frowned. "Don't pretend this is something it isn't."

"You make the whole idea seem like torture. Is Gus so bad?"

He was perfect. *You don't really know that*, her rational mind countered. *Those rules you agreed to are no guarantee he won't break your heart.*

"This has nothing to do with Gus, and you know it.

You strong-armed us when you know I'm not dating right now."

Polly snorted. "I've been hearing about that since you and Larry broke up months ago. And Gus... He hasn't had a date in forever, either. Don't you think it's high time you both climbed back in the saddle?"

Wanda crossed her arms. "I can't speak for Gus, but I agreed not to meddle in your private business anymore. I'd appreciate you not meddling in mine."

"Fair enough. Let me say one more thing. Gus is a fine man any woman would be proud to be out with. Later, you'll thank me for this."

~

THURSDAY NIGHT, as nervous as she could ever remember being for a date—even if this wasn't a real one—Wanda rescheduled her last appointment to get ready for Gus.

By eight-thirty, only she and Nadia remained at the salon.

"You don't need to stay," Wanda said. "Go on home."

"I will, but first, I want to see you in the outfit you brought."

The idea of showing up anyplace in town without her standard clothing and heels made Wanda un-comfortable, but she was ready to relax her stan-dards a bit. Casual clothes and boots seemed a good compromise. "All right, if you really want to wait around."

Ten minutes later, she stood before Nadia in a lime-green peasant blouse, pressed jeans that made her legs look longer and red leather cowboy boots with three-inch heels.

"You look amazing," Nadia said. "Larry will eat his heart out he if sees you."

"That'd be nice." Even if the thought of seeing him gave Wanda hives. Facing him wasn't exactly at the top of her to-do list.

"You're not having second thoughts about him, are you?"

"I wouldn't take him back on a sterling silver platter."

"Excellent. Gus is the better man in every way. Better looking, smarter and a whole lot nicer. Who knows, this non-date" —Nadia made air quotes around that— "could turn your life in a brand-new direction. You and Gus could become a thing." She fanned herself with both hands. "Wouldn't that be something?"

"You sound like Rochelle, Polly and everyone at the salon." Word of Wanda's non-date with Gus had spread like wildfire, and it seemed the entire town knew. "For the zillionth time, we're only doing this because Polly forced our hands," Wanda grumbled.

"As long as you're going out, you may as well enjoy yourself," Nadia advised. "Can't wait to hear all about it. See you tomorrow." She blew a kiss and left.

Wanda locked the cash register, rinsed out the coffee pots, tidied the magazines in the waiting area, and otherwise readied the salon for the following morning.

At nine sharp, twin headlights flashed through the closed blinds. Gus pulled right up to the door. She'd barely fluffed her hair and tugged her blouse over her hips before he strode in.

On this last day of April the weather had turned, and the air that swept in with him was warm.

"Hey," he said. In faded jeans and a "Firefighters

Are Hot" T-shirt, he was handsome as sin. But then, he could wear a floor-length poncho and be just gorgeous.

He ran an approving gaze from her head to her boots. "You look good."

Her insides quivered. "Thanks."

She doused all but the security lights, leaving the salon in semi-darkness. "Let me set the alarm, and we'll go."

As soon as she locked the door, she and Gus climbed into the Jeep and headed into the night.

17

As Gus drove through the darkness toward Marv's, Wanda sat silent and still as a statue —except for the fidgeting hands in her lap. He'd never seen her this uptight.

"Careful or you'll chew a hole in your bottom lip."

She relaxed her hold on the lip and glanced at him, the scant light from the tall poles along Kirkdale Road bathing her face in shadow. "I'm nervous."

"Not on my account, I hope."

"No."

"This is about Larry," he realized. And regretted not picking a different place to go. "Why don't we skip dessert and grab a drink somewhere else?"

"No way. I've been dreaming of a big slice of Marv's chocolate cream pie for days. I meant what I said. Larry doesn't matter anymore. But knowing I could come face-to-face with him is a little daunting." Her restless fingers clenched together.

"When was the last time you saw him?"

"In September. We hadn't spoken in days. I knew he was losing interest, so I drove over to his house in a crazy attempt to make him care. I caught him in bed with someone else." She worked her poor lip again.

"Apparently, he'd been seeing her the whole time he was supposed to be with me."

"Ouch," Gus said. "No wonder you broke up with him."

"That's what I *should* have done. Instead, like an idiot, I called him the next day and asked for another chance." She ducked her head, avoiding his eyes. "I got lucky...he turned me down."

That explained why she dreaded running into her ex. Gus wanted to deck the SOB. His hands tightened on the wheel. "Why didn't you tell me this before?"

"Would you share that story? I'm not proud of what I did." In a softer voice, she added, "You'd think I'd have learned from all the other times I made a fool of myself. But no."

"We've all done stuff we wish we hadn't. I sure have."

"Like what?"

He didn't have to think long to choose one. "Here's my most recent relationship screw-up. Denise, my last girlfriend, wanted to get married."

"Polly never mentioned that."

"She didn't know."

"Why didn't you tell her?"

"I just didn't. Then she had her stroke and everything changed."

"She had to come first and Denise didn't understand."

In the interest of fair play, Gus explained. "Actually, she offered to help in any way she could. She wanted to be there for me, but I broke up with her instead."

Wanda gave him a sideways look. "Because?"

"Even before the stroke, I'd planned to end the relationship. Denise rode my case about getting married, one too many times. I got claustrophobic."

"Then she wasn't the right woman for you."

"Nope." Gus couldn't believe he was sharing his private stuff with Wanda. Opening up made his shoulders tight. In an effort to ease the tension, he rolled them, and then dug the biggest skeleton out of his closet. "The same thing has happened with other girlfriends, often enough that I'm starting to doubt I'll ever fall in love, let alone get married."

"You've never been in love?"

"I don't think so."

"I have. Every time I start a new relationship, I'm sure he's the right man for me and that eventually, we'll get married. Ha. That's why I made my dating plan—to keep me from repeating stupid mistakes and getting in over my head."

"Smart. You've had some bad luck."

"Is that what you call it?" Her shoulders slumped and her head bowed. "Sometimes I wonder if I'm worth loving at all."

Her voice was so low, he wasn't sure he heard correctly. Couldn't believe flirty, sexy Wanda felt this way. Suddenly the bright, colorful clothes and makeup made sense. She used them to hide her insecurities.

He shook his head. "We make quite a pair."

WANDA COULDN'T BELIEVE she'd disclosed her biggest fear to Gus. A fear she rarely admitted even to herself, and had never divulged to anyone. But driving along in the darkness, commiserating their failures in love, made her feel safe, as if they'd forged a bond of trust.

When they parked and headed toward the door of

Marv's, anxiety replaced the safe feeling. She wished she'd kept her mouth shut. "What I told you...don't repeat it."

"I won't. The same goes for me."

"I would never."

"We'll shake on it." Gus extended his arm.

They shook hands, which made her laugh.

"She finally smiles." Looking pleased with himself, he opened the door for her.

As usual, Marv's was busy and noisy. Country music from the old juke-box and conversation filled the air, while waitstaff scurried around, keeping the customers satisfied.

Gus found a table near the entrance. From here, Wanda could see the entire room. To her relief, she didn't spot Larry.

Karen, a middle-age waitress who'd worked at Marv's forever, hurried over. "Hello, Gus. Hi, Wanda. I like the dark-brown hair and platinum bands. Haven't seen either of you kids in ages. I didn't realize you knew each other. Do you need menus?"

Gus shook his head.

"Me, either," Wanda said. "Gus and I are friends," she added, to set the waitress straight.

He flashed his teeth at the waitress. "How you doin' tonight, Karen?"

"Busy as always. I do have some exciting news. I'm going to be a grandma."

"No kidding. Congrats."

Wanda added her own good wishes, then ordered chocolate cream pie and a glass of red wine. Gus asked for a burger, fries, and beer.

After Karen bustled off, he eyed Wanda. "Wine and chocolate pie?"

"Don't knock it until you've tried it. They're great together. But then, I'm a chocoholic."

"Figured you were."

His grin made her feel comfortable and relaxed. "Did you work on the Lincoln today?" she asked over the noise.

He nodded. "I lucked out and found most of the parts I've been looking for."

"That's cool. How did you manage that?"

"First I... You sure you want to hear about this? It's not an exciting story."

"Do you even have to ask?"

With that, he launched into the details.

"Soon, you'll have her shining inside and out," Wanda replied when he finished. "When do you think she'll be done?"

"A few weeks at most. I'll let you know when I post the photos."

"Do you have another job lined up?"

"Not yet, but the next car will come along. They always do. How was your day?"

"Normal. Styling hair, coloring hair, chitchat."

"I could never do your job. The customers would look like plucked chickens."

She pictured that and smiled. "Any fires this week?"

"A bad one early Tuesday morning, caused by a space heater too close to a blanket. It was cold that night, remember? A mom and two little girls."

Wanda shuddered. "Are they okay?"

"We got them all out of the duplex where they lived, thank God. But they lost almost everything, and they don't have renter's insurance."

Her heart went out to them. "What are they going to do?"

"Our benefit fund will help some. As much as I disliked posing for the calendar, at times like this, I'm proud to have participated."

He was such a good man, and she admired him so much. "I'm doubly glad I bought extra calendars for my mom and sister. I'd like to contribute more."

"I thought you were saving your quarters to buy the salon."

"I still want to help. Don't forget, I'm going to earn a bundle from that bridal party. Donating part of that to a worthy cause won't mess up my budget at all. That reminds me, if you know of any brides-to-be looking for a stylist, I'm your woman."

"My woman, huh?"

Gus's eyes glinted and her body went on high alert. She crossed her legs and ignored the tingling. "Your woman *hair-stylist*," she clarified.

Just then, she spotted Larry...and he saw her. The lively conversation had temporarily erased any apprehension about seeing him. Tension flooded back, tying her stomach in knots.

Her expression must have tipped off Gus. He glanced over his shoulder. "I assume that's Larry?"

"Unfortunately."

Lanky and self-assured, he sauntered toward Wanda with the smile that had once made her heart pound.

Not anymore.

Gus scooted his chair close enough that his leg pressed hers. Steady and reassuring.

"Hey, baby," Larry drawled. "Lookin' good. Real good."

Gus settled his arm possessively around her shoulders. "Get lost, buddy. She's my woman now."

Her ex lost some of his swagger.

Gus's behavior was all for show, but to Wanda, it felt real, as if she really was his woman.

She went soft and her heart expanded with feelings. Hardly aware of her actions, she rested her hand on Gus's massive thigh. Under her palm a muscle twitched. She started to move away, but he clamped his big hand over hers, trapping her against that solid warmth.

With Larry looking on, Gus tipped up her chin with his free hand and kissed her. Lightly at first, then deeper. Hot and passionate, promising even more.

Wanda forgot she was in a public place, forgot that, for her own good, she needed to stop. All that mattered was Gus.

When he pulled away and her eyes fluttered open, Larry was gone.

"That takes care of that," she said, striving to sound normal instead of highly-stimulated.

"I broke the rules," Gus said.

Rules? Wanda struggled to remember. That's right, they'd agreed to several. "You helped me out, so it's okay."

If she didn't count the heat melting her insides.

Karen chose that moment to deliver their food and drink. "Just friends, huh?" she said with a knowing grin.

No reaction from Gus. "Thanks for the food, Karen."

"MYOB. Got it. Enjoy." With a wink, she hurried off.

Instead of returning to his place, Gus stayed close.

Wanda considered scooting her chair away, but the damage had been done. She was also starving, and his burger and fries smelled heavenly. Especially the fries.

"As usual, they served enough fries for four guys.

Help yourself." Gus squirted a generous dollop of ketchup on the side of the plate.

Feigning lightheartedness she didn't feel, Wanda smiled. "I thought you'd never ask."

Conversation ceased while they dug in. Then Gus squinted at her. "You okay about Larry?"

She nodded. "Thanks for getting rid of him."

"My pleasure." His hot eyes turned her to mush. "The guy's a total loser for letting you go."

He shouldn't say things like that. Wanda told herself it didn't mean anything, but her heart disagreed. And not just a little bit. The wayward thing had moved totally into Gus's corner.

For all her caution and worry, the worst had happened. She'd fallen head over heels for Gus, sinking deeper into love with his every warm glance and kind word.

She was his.

Which meant she'd probably end up in a world of hurt. If she had even a shred of pride, she would never let him know.

Oblivious, he stuffed a fry into his mouth and chewed with gusto. Lovesickness had ruined her appetite. As upset as she was with herself, she no longer wanted food. Could barely look at the pie.

Misunderstanding, he chuckled. "Help me out here. I don't want to waste anything."

He dipped a fry in ketchup and fed it to her with a tender sweetness no man had ever shown her before.

With that, the last, fraying shreds of common sense snapped. What would be would be. And Wanda wanted it all, regardless of the consequences.

Gus coaxed her to taste his burger, then teased her when she closed her eyes and moaned over its deliciousness. Wanda managed to keep up her end of the conversation but couldn't have recalled a word to save her life. She was too caught up in sensations. The heat of his leg against hers. His mesmerizing, deep voice. The way he swallowed his food. How he looked at her, as if no one else mattered.

By the time he finished his meal, she was a seething tangle of love and longing.

"Aren't you gonna eat your pie?" he said.

"Your food filled me up," she said. "Go ahead. Try it with a sip of wine."

He made a face but passed her his fork. "Dish me up, woman."

Loving that he referred to her again as woman, she speared him a huge bite. Gus opened his mouth and leaned forward to take it. With his eyes locked on hers, he licked the tines clean.

She could almost feel the stroke of his tongue on her skin. Her nipples hardened. She had no idea what he desired in a lifetime partner or if he even wanted one, but she knew what he wanted tonight. Her.

She wanted him, too.

His eyelids dropped to half-mast. "What are we doing here, Wanda?"

Going up in flames. "Y-you're tasting my pie. While that chocolate taste lingers in your mouth, drink the wine."

He sipped, then smacked his lips. "Not bad."

"Told you."

"Your turn."

Using the same fork, he fed her again, easing the pie slowly into her mouth. As seductive as foreplay—the best foreplay of her life.

For all Wanda knew, the pie tasted like dirt. She wanted Gus more than she could ever remember wanting a man. Even more than Wayne in those first months after she'd lost her virginity.

He flirted with a frown. "There's something different about you, something I can't quite put my finger on."

"I want to be alone with you," she admitted, no longer able to pretend otherwise.

His eyes smoldered. "Do you mean that?"

She nodded.

The fork clattered against the pie plate. He tossed a few bills on the table and stood. "Let's get out of here."

18

Holding tight to Wanda's hand, Gus tugged her through the parking lot. The urge to kiss her wouldn't let go. In the shadows near the Jeep, he ravaged her mouth.

He tasted chocolate and wine and a special something uniquely hers. Standing on her toes, she pressed her sweet curves closer. His body ignited. If they didn't stop, he would lose control and take her right here against the car.

That was not an option. Mustering control, he broke away. She wore the dazed look he was beginning to crave.

He needed to touch her the way he needed air. His fingers trailed down her smooth cheek. "Your place is a good twenty minutes away. Mine is closer."

"Yours, then."

Moments later, as he eased the Jeep toward the exit, Wanda glanced at him. "I should probably pick up the Civic at the salon and follow you, but I don't want to take the time."

Nor did he. "We'll worry about that later."

She nodded. "Are you clean?"

"Yep. You?"

"Yes, but I'm not on birth control pills anymore."

"What do you use instead?"

"At the moment, nothing." She shifted in her seat. "I haven't had sex in eight months."

"It's been almost a year for me."

Even in the darkness, he noted her widened eyes. "I didn't realize a man could go that long."

"It isn't easy, but sometimes life rolls that way."

"But a man like you can get any woman you want."

More than a few females had propositioned him. "I haven't wanted anyone. Until you."

"I'm the same. Do you have protection?"

Gus thought about the box of condoms he'd bought after that morning at the garage—just in case —and nodded.

Eager to get to his place, he kept an eye out for cops and stayed at the top end of the speed limit. He pulled into the lot of his apartment complex, then eased the Jeep into his reserved slot.

During the short walk into the building and on the interminable elevator ride to the third floor, he managed to keep his hands off her. But the second he ushered her into his place, he kicked the door shut and pushed her against it. Pinned her hands over her head and kissed her.

Forget slow and gentle. He demanded. She met him with equal passion. With his free hand, he cupped her breast.

Moaning, she thrust out her chest and pressed tight against his hard-on. Wriggling and hungry, killing him.

His breathing ragged, he released her wrists to grasp her hips and hold her still. "I want you in my bed, Wanda. But I don't want you to regret this later. Your plan and all."

"Tonight, there is no plan." She reached for him again.

He lifted her up. Her thighs wrapped around his hips. She stretched up and placed a damp kiss on the underside of his jaw.

Gus strode rapidly down the hall carrying Wanda in his massive arms, as if she weighed nothing. The furious thud of Gus's heart pounded against her ear. Her own beat just as hard.

In the bedroom, he flipped a switch and the bedside lamp flared to brilliance. Tan walls and an impressive dark-wood headboard personified masculinity. A tidy bedspread covered the king-size bed.

"You made your bed." A little suspicious, she eyed him. "Were you planning on bringing me back here?"

"Not at all. I always make my bed."

"Polly," she guessed.

"Also my dad and the department. At the station, I'm required to keep a neat bed and strip it clean when I leave."

"I had no idea firefighters were such sticklers for tidiness and promptness."

Gus kissed her and she forgot everything except the man in her arms.

He removed the spread with one hand. Wanda had no idea where he put it. He set her down, at the edge of the tautly-stretched blanket. Kneeling on the carpet at her feet, he pulled off her boots and socks, his swiftness betraying his eagerness. Next, he unbuttoned her jeans and tugged the zipper down. She lifted one hip, then the other, allowing him to peel her jeans down and off.

He sat on his heels for a moment. "Red bikinis— nice."

They, too, disappeared.

He spread her thighs apart. Did he notice she was already wet for him?

Cool air rushed over her feverish skin, followed by the sensual whisper of warm breath. Then....Nothing.

"What are you doing?" she asked, impatient.

"Looking at you. You're real pretty, Wanda."

No one had ever complimented this part of her. "Is that supposed to be a joke?"

"I mean it." He slid her closer and got down to business.

He'd barely touched his wicked tongue to her most sensitive part before she went over the edge in a shuddering climax.

When she went limp, he glanced up at her with a wicked grin. "That was quick."

"Because it's been a long time." And never as good as this.

"I won't lose control as fast. I've wanted you for a while, and I'm going to make this last."

He joined her on the bed. Kissed her mouth. She tasted herself on his tongue and hovered on the verge of another climax.

Wanting to hold back and return the favor, she reached for the tented fly of his jeans.

"No, Wanda." Gus jerked and lifted her hand away. "This is all about you."

"Me?" Confused, she frowned. "But what about you? You've waited longer than me."

"I'll keep. Tell me what you like."

"I don't understand. What about your likes?"

"Making you feel good heightens my pleasure."

"How can that be true?"

"Because it is. Not giving you pleasure would make me a sorry excuse of a man."

No one had ever put her first. Love flooded her until she was bursting with it. "Gus Viggio, you're one in a million."

"I'm just a guy who wants to satisfy his woman."

His woman. There it was again.

"Am I your woman?" she asked boldly. In the hope that maybe, just maybe he wanted more than sex...

"Tonight, you are."

Nope, only sex. At least he was honest.

With a sound of pure male lust, he removed the rest of her clothing. When she lay naked before him, he worked his way down her body, taking his time touching and tasting and exploring.

A novel experience that thrilled her.

"I don't know what you like," he reminded her.

With his tongue lapping her nipple, speaking wasn't easy. "Anything is fine."

"Tell me," he growled.

"What you're doing is pretty darned amazing."

"I'm enjoying it, too." He returned to the task at hand.

Later, trusting him fully—at least here in bed—she let him know what turned her on. He paid attention and took her to the brink again and again without release, until she was frantic with need.

"What else do you want?" he asked, his voice hoarse with desire.

"You, inside me. Now."

"Thank you, God."

In a blink, he stripped. With astonishment, she realized he'd been waiting for her okay.

He stood over her, gloriously aroused. Huge and jutting. Such a beautiful man. She sucked in a breath.

Misinterpreting, he frowned down at himself. "Yeah, I know I'm on the big side. Don't worry, I'll take it nice and easy, so that you have time to adjust." He joined her on the bed.

"Oh, I'm not complaining," she said, wetting her lips. "I'm excited."

She wrapped her arms around him and kissed him thoroughly.

Skin on skin. Heaven.

Aching and beyond ready, she broke the kiss. "Where's that protection?"

"Bedside table. Hang tight."

He left her and returned with a foil packet in hand.

"Give that to me, Gus."

He handed over the condom.

"On your back," she said, feeling sexy and powerful.

She took her time, rolling the condom down his length and sneaking in extra strokes.

His hands fisted at his sides, jerking the blanket loose and hissing.

"Are you okay?" she teased.

"I will be if you hurry up."

The instant she finished sheathing him, he flipped her onto her back. Supporting his weight on his arms, he covered her with his body.

With his teeth gritted, he inched inside, pausing before he went far. "How's that?"

"Too slow."

"I don't want to hurt you."

She raised her hips, forcing him deeper. "Making me wait is painful."

"Bossy, aren't you? I aim to please."

One thrust and he went in deep, stretching her to her limits.

"Okay?" he asked.

"So okay. More."

Somehow he pushed in deeper still. Wanda moaned. "Oh, dear God, that's incredible. Please, Gus. Faster."

"I thought I was turned on before," he murmured, his arms corded with the effort of holding back. "But this...you..."

She leaned up and nipped his neck. He shut up and gave her what she craved. Friction, hard, fast, deep, until she exploded in wave after wave of pleasure.

When she finally floated down to earth, she felt thoroughly satisfied. Whole, complete. Utterly under his spell, for as long as he wanted her.

And scared witless for the time when the excitement of new sex faded and he broke her heart.

19

S pent and relaxed, Gus flopped onto his pillow. "That was off the charts."

He'd figured it would be, but wow.

"Mm-hmm," Wanda murmured beside him, sounding drowsy and content.

He turned off the lamp, propped his head on his arms, and stared up at the dark ceiling. She'd been so adamant about sticking to her plan, he'd never anticipated ending the evening like this.

What had changed her mind?

As he thought back over the evening, he realized her attitude had shifted after the kiss he'd laid on her for Larry's benefit. From what she'd said, her ex and all the other men in her life, including her own father, had treated her poorly.

Each and every one of the bastards deserved a seat in hell. A decent man ought to treat a woman with respect. Gus had done that without expecting anything in return. Yeah, he'd wanted sex, but he'd agreed to abide by the rules they both needed but had quickly abandoned.

All because he'd played nice.

He wasn't. As much as he liked Wanda, and he

liked her a lot, it wouldn't last. No matter how strong his feelings tonight or how fantastic the sex.

Damned if he wanted his name added to the list of jerks who'd broken her heart. He didn't want to hurt her, ever, but with his track record, that seemed inevitable.

Royally pissed at himself for bringing her to his bed, he knew what he needed to do. Warn her to get out fast, while the damage was minimal. He turned to her and cleared his throat.

Oblivious of his intentions, she released a sleepy sigh, rose up and kissed the place over his unreliable heart. Between her lips on his chest and her soft breasts brushing his skin, his brain clouded.

To hell with the future. This was all that mattered.

Desperate to taste her mouth, he tipped her chin and indulged. The smoldering kiss quickly flared to inferno level.

"Stay right where you are while I get the protection," she whispered in the darkness.

"You can't see a thing. I'll get it."

Moments later, he opened the foil packet.

"Hurry," she pleaded.

He started to flip her on her back, but she placed her hand on his pec. "My turn to be on top."

She straddled him and sank down, taking him fully into her warmth.

God, she felt good. Gus's eyes crossed. He raised his hips and pushed in as far as he could. This time, he meant to go slow and prolong the pleasure, but she was too eager and he was too hot for her.

After another spectacular climax, they fell asleep holding each other.

Sometime later, she woke him. Groggy, he rubbed his eyes. "What time is it?"

"One-thirty. I don't think I should stay the night."

That was probably for the best, but dog that he was, Gus didn't want to let her go. He tightened his arms around her and nuzzled the sensitive place beneath her ear. "Don't leave yet."

"But my car is at the salon," she protested, angling her head to give him more access.

"Right."

He couldn't seem to get enough. Cupping her breast, he played his thumb across her hardening nipple. She rewarded him with a longing moan.

"If you take me to get it in the morning, everyone will know we spent the night together," she said, sounding breathless.

"Would that be so bad?"

She smacked him playfully and scooted out of reach. "This was supposed to be a non-date, remember? If I don't get my car tonight, rumors will fly."

"Be assured, they already are. As long as we enjoy each other's company, what we do in private is no one else's business."

"Yes, but... It's hard to put my thoughts into words."

What was she getting at? Clueless, he flipped on the bedside table lamp, then blinked in the sudden light. "We'll get up early and I'll drive you to the salon before it opens. No one will be the wiser."

She hesitated. He fiddled with her hair, combing his hands through it and smoothing the bangs out of her eyes. Last night he'd learned she liked that. "Stay."

"You want sex again?"

"Definitely." He slid his hand between her legs. She was already wet. "So do you."

"Wait." Her thighs slammed shut, forcing him to stop. "Is that all you want?"

The playful smile didn't quite reach her eyes, but he was too focused on getting inside her to think much about it. He glanced at his erection and let out a soft laugh. "I won't lie, sex is a big part of what I want. But I also like having you in my bed. The thought of waking up beside you... I can't think of a better way to start the day."

Her big eyes lit with warmth.

"We good now?" He kissed her eyelids closed, then settled on her mouth for a long, deep kiss.

After that, there were no more questions.

GUS WOKE BEFORE DAWN. He could've used a couple extra hours' rest, but he never had been able to sleep in. His empty belly prodded him to get up. Man, was he hungry.

Despite fatigue and starvation, he felt on top of the world. Last night had blown his mind—every time he and Wanda had sex, which was a bunch. Remembering, he smiled at the passionate, beautiful woman sleeping beside him. Make that half-sprawled on top of him.

In the darkness he couldn't see her face, but he felt her sweet breath skim across his chest. A wave of tenderness washed over him.

In so many ways, they matched up. Passion, enthusiasm, wit, smarts—you name it. Each time they made love, his desire for her grew.

Hard and ready, he considered another round of hot sex. But Wanda was anxious to get her car. He cupped her shoulder. "Hey."

She didn't budge, not even when he moved out from under her. "It's time to get your car."

"Mmph." Turning away from him, she burrowed under the covers.

"You wanted to pick it up super early," he reminded her.

She pulled the pillow over her head.

Gus left the bed. Made a lot of noise opening dresser drawers for clean clothes. Nothing roused her.

She obviously needed the rest. Shrugging, he headed into the bathroom, showered, shaved and dressed.

When he reentered the bedroom, she was still out cold.

Well, he'd tried. Leaving the door open, he padded barefoot into the kitchen, where he started the coffee maker. Moments later, he poured himself the first mug of the day. With an eye on the wall clock, he sat down with the latest edition of the Guff's Lake News.

He glanced at the headlines but couldn't focus on the articles. If Wanda wanted to get to the salon ahead of everyone, she needed to get up. Five more minutes, then he'd wake her even if she resisted.

For all he knew, she'd changed her mind and decided not to worry about the car. Hell, she might even want breakfast.

How would she feel in the light of day? He rooted through the fridge and pulled out ingredients. Would she regret last night?

In a few minutes, he'd find out.

20

Wanda woke up sore in all the right places from lots of really great sex. She'd never been with a man as passionate and considerate as Gus. And bonus: he didn't push her away when she wanted to snuggle. Speaking of snuggling... Facing away from him and craving his touch, she scooted backward toward his warmth. She met with emptiness.

He wasn't in bed.

Daylight shone through a chink in the drapes. She glanced at the clock. Eight a.m. Darn it! He'd promised to wake her.

She bolted upright, threw her legs over the edge of the bed and stood. She really needed a shower, but getting to her car posthaste took precedence over hygiene.

After using the facilities, she threw on the only clothes she had—the blouse, jeans and underwear from last night. Yuck. She ran a quick comb through her tangled mess of hair, for all the good that did. It needed washing and styling. She looked really bad, but that couldn't be helped.

At a fast clip, she exited the bedroom. The heady aroma of bacon and coffee filled the air. Her mouth watered.

Gus stood barefoot at the stove, wielding a fork over a pan of sizzling bacon. In jeans and a faded Coldplay T-shirt, he looked big, badass and gorgeous.

Ignoring the urge to launch herself into his arms, Wanda shoved her hands into her jeans pockets. Not wanting to sound naggy or mad, which would cause conflict, a definite no-no, she kept her voice light. "You were supposed to wake me."

"Trust me, I tried to a couple times. You're a sound sleeper. I was getting ready to bring you a coffee but figured I'd start cooking breakfast first. Here."

He grabbed a mug from the cabinet, placed it in her hands and pointed to the coffee-maker.

He'd planned to serve her coffee in bed and then feed her? Aww.

But she had more pressing things on her mind. "It's too late to sneak me to my car. Everyone will know we spent the night together."

"So?"

She paused to add milk and sugar to her coffee, which Gus had set out for her. A lot of both, as the stuff was strong enough to put hair on her chest. "This is a big deal, Gus. I must have explained about our non-date umpteen times. People will think I lied or that I ditched my plan. Either way, I look weak."

"Weak," he repeated, shaking his head.

"That's right. Wishy-washy behavior is unattractive."

"First, you're super attractive. Second, name me one person who hasn't had a weak moment or three. No big deal."

Wanda didn't believe a single word.

"With your strong personality, no one could possibly consider you wishy-washy," Gus added.

He thought she was strong? She wasn't. "Quit trying to sweet-talk me."

"I mean it." He put his arm around her and kissed the tip of her nose. "Who cares what anyone else thinks?"

Was he serious? "I do!" She ducked out of his grasp.

Hands up, he stepped back. "There's no reason to get bent out of shape over this. Even if I'd taken you to get your car at dawn, someone could have spotted us. Anyway, it's too late now. You may as well relax. I need food, and I'll bet you're just as hungry."

On cue, her stomach gurgled loudly, urging her to feed it. Last night's activities had worked up a powerful appetite.

"What'd I tell you?" He pointed the cooking fork at her. "After we eat, we'll drive to your house. You can get ready for work, then I'll drop you at the salon. "

"Me getting out of your car... Oh, that's going to help."

"Relax. Everything will be fine. Are you sorry you stayed over? I'm not."

His heavy-lidded look dissolved her worries and caused havoc inside her. She didn't regret a single second their night together. "It was wonderful, Gus."

Still, regardless of the sweet things he'd said in the throes of passion, she had no idea how to keep him happy. No idea when he'd start feeling claustrophobic or tire of her.

He added the last of the crisp bacon to a paper towel-covered plate. "How do you like your eggs?"

With a resigned sigh, she plunked onto one of the stools at the eating bar. "Scrambled, and could I have toast, too?"

"You bet."

Before long, Gus set two plates on the bar and then sat beside her.

Despite her misgivings, she enjoyed every morsel.

AN HOUR AND CHANGE LATER, Gus drove Wanda to work. She sure spent a long time on her hair and makeup.

Decked out in a form-fitting blue dress, lacy tights and blue contact lenses, she pulled down her visor, glanced in the attached mirror and deftly applied red-orange lipstick. Camouflage she didn't need.

"Do I look okay?" she asked.

"Yes, but I like you better naked."

"Spoken like a man."

"Guilty as charged."

She put the visor up, donned her shades, settled against the seat and stared out the window. Spring was in full fledge, with flowers dotting the green meadows on both sides of the road. The bright sun promised another warm day, not unusual for early May.

"This is my favorite season," he said.

"Mine, too. When we get to the salon, could you pull around back?"

She was still worried about being seen together. Gus shrugged. "If that's what you want."

She nodded and went quiet again.

"You're not like most women," he noted as he braked at a light.

"Because I asked you to stop around back? You know my reasons."

"Not that. You don't force a conversation."

"If you'd rather, I'll chat away."

"Just be yourself."

"Even I know what a big bore that is."

Gus snorted. "Where'd you get an idea like that?"

"Cindy."

Her own mom? He couldn't believe it. The light turned green, and he headed forward. "She doesn't really think you're boring."

"She absolutely does, and she's right. That's why she pushed me to be different. I'm glad she did, because when I finally bought in, the changes I made worked wonders."

"I don't follow."

"I told you about Cindy's husbands and all the boyfriends. When my sister copied Cindy's behavior, she suddenly had tons of dates and her pick of boyfriends. Cindy didn't want me to be the lonely girl everyone felt sorry for, and neither did I.

"The summer before high school, she helped me reinvent myself. She taught me how to dress and wear makeup, and shared everything she knew about pleasing a man. Well, not the sex, but everything else. It worked, and my life changed dramatically."

Another piece of the puzzle that was Wanda clicked into place. Gus pictured her as a little girl and her mom harping on her to stop being herself. The woman sounded like a character out of a bad movie. And he thought he'd had it rough.

He shook his head. "No disrespect meant toward Cindy, but it sounds as if she did a real number on you."

"At times, she does come on a little strong, but I can't imagine where I'd be without her help."

She'd probably like herself better, but Gus knew better than to say so. "You were yourself at the garage and again last night," he said. "You seemed happy, and you sure pleased me."

"You mean good sex."

"Superior sex," he corrected, grinning. "Also the talk and the laughs. I enjoy being with you."

Realizing he was starting to sound like a guy on the brink of a relationship, he shut his mouth.

"Of course you do. For now," she said. "I know how men operate. Once the heat of those first frenzied weeks of passion dies down, feelings also cool."

"Care to test that theory on me?" Had he just said that? The crazy part was, he meant it. Damn.

She looked as surprised as he felt. "Relationships give you claustrophobia. Besides, I don't even know what you really want. How can I possibly make you happy?"

Hell if Gus knew. All he cared about was spending more time with her. Might as well lay his cards on the table.

"We both have our issues, and we're both gun-shy," he agreed. "But these past few weeks, this thing between us... I don't know what it is, but I'd like to find out."

Her big eyes widened as if she were spooked. "You're right, we could run into a wall and part company," he went on. "Or we could move the opposite direction. We'll never know unless we try."

"You're asking me to ditch my plan," she said, gnawing the pad of her thumb.

"Temporarily, if that makes you feel better."

Wanda didn't say another word until he pulled to a

stop behind the salon. "I need time to think about this."

"No rush. Call me when you decide."

She nodded. Started to reach for the door handle. Hesitated, then swiveled to face him again. Leaning across the bucket seats, she kissed him.

He took that as a favorable sign.

Reeling from Gus's startling proposal that they get involved, Wanda entered the salon.

"Hey there," Tommie greeted. "Your Civic was here when I opened this morning."

Outed as soon as she stepped through the door. Wanda froze.

"I thought maybe you'd come in for an early appointment," the salon owner went on. "But this is the first I've seen of you. You and Gus went out after work, right?"

"On a non-date," Wanda reminded her with a nonchalance she didn't feel.

"Did your car stall?"

"Um, no."

"Then what?" Tommie asked, all tell me.

Stylists and customers added their own curious expressions.

Not about to add fuel to that fire, Wanda held up her brown-bag lunch. "I should put this in the fridge before my appointment arrives."

Tommie didn't pry further. Wanda had barely released a relieved breath before Carol Sue started in.

"It's all over town that you and Gus had a very

good time at Marv's last night," she chirped, almost rubbing her hands in anticipation.

Wanda smiled sweetly. "Who wouldn't have fun over drinks and chocolate cream pie?"

"Feeding and kissing each other does sound fun."

Heat climbed Wanda's neck and face. "I really need to put my food away."

She hurried toward the kitchen.

As she reached for the Employees Only door, Nadia snagged her arm. "I don't have a customer for another half hour," she murmured in a voice only Wanda could hear. "What happened?"

Rochelle joined them. "Mrs. Alberts will be under the dryer for a while yet. I can spare a few minutes."

Wanda wanted to tell them everything, but that required more time than she had. "Not me. My noon appointment should be here any second."

When she returned to the salon some minutes later, everyone had gone back to business. For the rest of the day no one commented, but the hushed whispers and knowing looks were hard to ignore.

What had she expected, when Carol Sue had broadcast her behavior with Gus to a T? If only they hadn't fed each other within sight of the whole restaurant. Kissing at the table hadn't been so bright, either, even if it had gotten rid of Larry.

Wanda didn't get a chance to talk privately with her friends until hours later, when they synchronized a quick break and sat down at the table in the employees' kitchen.

"You spent a whole night with Gus," Nadia said, after she filled them in.

"Please keep your voice down," Wanda cautioned.

Rochelle shook her head and spoke softly. "I can't even imagine. I'll bet he's great in bed."

Wanda leaned in and lowered her voice to just above a whisper. "It was incredible."

Nadia placed both hands over her heart. "You and that big hunk of man... I'm so jealous."

Rochelle just smiled. "If Matt and I weren't dating, I would be, too."

Her dreamy expression said it all. "You really like him," Wanda guessed.

"More than any guy in ages. We don't want to rush into anything, but we're already talking about the future." She looked radiant.

Rochelle didn't have any hang-ups about taking a chance on love. Wanda envied her.

"Could you save the Matt stuff for later?" Nadia said. "We don't have much time, and I want to hear about Gus."

Wanda filled them in, ending with Gus's suggestion that they try a relationship.

"What did you tell him?" Nadia asked.

"Nothing yet. He caught me totally off-guard. I said I'd think about it. I'm not sure what to do."

"Excuse me, but you and Gus kissed at Marv's, then spent a fabulous night together. What's left to figure out?" Nadia asked.

Wanda sighed. "He kissed me to get rid of Larry when he stopped at our table. Yes, we slept together, but that doesn't mean I want to set my plan aside. I'm not ready to give it up."

Comprehension dawned on Rochelle's face. "Now I understand. That plan is your safety net."

Stunned, Wanda sat back hard in her chair. "Oh, my God, you're right. I never realized. How did you?"

"It makes sense. For a while, your plan worked for you. But things change. From where I sit, you don't need that safety net anymore. Because let's get real here—you and Gus are already involved."

Wanda groaned and massaged her temples.

"Don't listen to her." Nadia gave Rochelle a dirty look before turning to Wanda. "This is your life. If you want to hold on to your plan, go ahead. Just answer me this. Do you want to be with Gus?"

"Yes, but—"

"There's your answer."

"Let me finish," Wanda said. "I don't know how to keep him happy or hold his interest later. We all know what that means—in the end, he'll walk away. Don't forget, his past relationships haven't worked out any better than mine. He's never even been in love." Even saying the words made her heart ache.

"That doesn't mean he won't fall in love with you," Nadia argued.

"True, but there's no guarantee that he will. I'm super scared of getting hurt again. I wish I knew the right thing to do."

Rochelle looked thoughtful. "As I see it, you have two options. Take a risk and go for the man you want or play it safe and stay away from him because you're afraid you might end up with a broken heart. The safe route is also a risk—of losing the chance to be happy with Gus."

Nadia nodded. "I couldn't have said it better. If it were me, I'd jump into this relationship with both feet and enjoy whatever happens for as long as it lasts."

"When he grows tired of me, then what?" Wanda hugged herself.

Nadia frowned. "You can't be certain that will happen. Gus isn't like the men you usually date. He's a great guy, and he wants to be with you."

Tommie poked her head into the room. "Nadia,

your five o'clock is here. Wanda, Patsy Jones is on the phone about her wedding, and Rochelle, Matt is out front, waiting to take you to dinner. I'm ready to call it a day."

They all stood, leaving the conversation unfinished and Wanda undecided.

PLAY safe or take a chance with Gus? Nearly a week later, Wanda was still wavering. The man had actually listened and stayed away since Friday, giving her the space she'd asked for. For that alone, he stood head and shoulders above the rest.

But leaving her be was no insurance against breaking her heart.

She glanced out the window. And there he was, helping Polly from the Jeep for her weekly appointment.

He must have sensed her staring, for he looked straight at her. At least she assumed so. His dark sunglasses prevented her from knowing for sure.

The sunglasses came off when he ushered Polly through the door.

Aware that people were watching, Wanda avoided smoothing her caramel-color, gold-streaked hair and greeted them with her usual smile.

"Hey," Gus said.

"Good morning, Wanda. I need to powder my nose. I'll just be a moment." Polly turned toward the bathrooms.

"How are you?" Gus asked Wanda.

"Still thinking."

"That's cool."

His hot eyes belied the words and made her knees go weak, but he didn't pressure her.

"Tell my aunt I'll see her in forty-five."

Long minutes later, Polly returned. "Where did Gus go?"

"No idea, but he said he'll be back in forty-five minutes to pick you up."

"Has he asked you out since the last time?"

Wanda shook her head.

"That's a shame. I had so hoped the two of you would hit it off."

If she only knew. "Let's get you fixed up," Wanda said brightly.

She washed Polly's hair and set to work on the trim.

"You're awfully quiet today," Polly commented.

"Am I?" Wanda forced a lighthearted tone. "I guess I'm distracted."

"By what?"

Gus and her decision. "I'd rather not say."

"Of course." Looking disappointed, Polly opened her mouth.

Before she could pose another nosy question, Wanda changed the subject. "Did I tell you about the wedding party I'm doing next week? A bride and six bridesmaids."

She launched into details of the big to-do and easily distracted Polly.

Exactly forty-five minutes later, Gus collected his aunt.

Sometime after lunch, Wanda reached a decision. Scared half to death and in desperate need of a few moments alone, she headed for the door. "I need a pick-me-up before my next appointment," she explained, gesturing toward Sweet Nothings, the candy and ice cream shop at the opposite end of the street.

She wasn't lying. The salon's usual chocolate stash had disappeared hours ago, and she needed more. A lot more—even if her stomach clenched and her tight throat made swallowing difficult.

Seconds after she exited the building, Nadia and Rochelle fell into step beside her.

"It's so bright out here, I'm almost squinting in my shades," Nadia said. "I can't believe you're not wearing any."

Wanda had been too distracted to notice.

"If you want candy this bad, you must be upset," Rochelle commented. "Let me guess, you decided not to take Gus up on his offer. Your choice, but I can't believe you're going to turn him down."

"No male has ever looked at me the way he looked at you today," Nadia said with envy. "You're going to break that man's heart. It's only fair to tell him right away."

Wanda pulled them both to a stop. "I'm shaking in my mules." She tucked her ice-cold hands under her arms. "I've been thinking about our conversation the other day. You're right. It's time for me to let go of my safety net. This is my chance at real love, and I can't allow fear to hold me back."

Nadia shared a triumphant grin with Rochelle.

"No fear!" They chanted in unison.

"No more fear," Wanda promised, willing it to be true. "Keep it to yourselves until I talk to Gus, okay? I'll call him after work."

She would figure out how to keep him happy for a long time, and never, ever back him into a corner and make him claustrophobic.

And if I fail? If he breaks my heart?

Despite the sun's warmth, a chill swept through her. Her shaking legs almost buckled. At least she would have taken the risk.

No more fear, she silently chided.

At Sweet Nothings, Wanda and her friends ordered ice cream cones. She left the shop with a double scoop chocolate mousse cone in hand, and the determination to move toward what she wanted. Without fear and without looking back.

22

At the tile counter in Polly's kitchen, Wanda stuffed the deviled eggs Polly had taught her to make.

She and Gus had arrived several hours earlier, along with Gus's father, Ed. The men to take care of the yard, and Wanda to get cooking lessons on making the eggs and frying chicken for this afternoon's Fourth of July picnic.

How could it already be July fourth? The last two months had flown by in a joyful blur. Sometimes she pinched herself to make sure this wasn't some wishful dream.

At other times... There had been moments when Gus seemed restless and she feared he was growing tired of her. Nothing she could quite put her finger on, just a funny feeling. Which was why she owned crotchless underwear, slinky lingerie and edible lotions to spice things up. Not that she needed the enhancements. With or without them, Gus reached for her with hunger and eagerness.

But for how much longer?

Her anxious stomach clenched. No fear, she silently scolded while she carefully arranged the eggs on a plate. *Look toward the future, not back at the past.* The words had become her mantra.

For all the brave pep-talk, she couldn't stem her longing to hear him say *I love you.* An iffy proposition, given that he'd never been in love before and had never promised to love her.

She wouldn't admit to loving him, either. No sense making him claustrophobic. She'd learned the hard way that saying the words first guaranteed the end of a relationship.

"How are those eggs coming?" Polly asked from her seat at the kitchen table. "I'm ready to wrap them in wax paper."

"Perfect timing. I just finished." Wanda carefully transported the plate to the table. "Ta-da!"

"They look marvelous, but the proof is in the taste. Don't mind if I do." Polly separated the two halves of an egg Wanda had pushed together and took a generous bite. After a moment, she nodded. "I couldn't have done a better job myself. And this is your first time making them. You're a natural."

High praise, indeed. Wanda beamed. "Thanks to your step-by-step instructions."

The back door opened. Ed clomped inside, followed by Gus. He shut it against the heat. Both men removed their work boots and left them near the door.

By now, Wanda had met Gus's father numerous times. She liked the friendly man. He was darker-skinned than Gus and about four inches shorter, but they shared the same killer smile.

Ed padded toward the powder room down the hall. Gus moved to the sink and washed his hands, then guzzled a glass of tap water.

"What do I see here?" Licking his lips, he wandered to the table.

"Deviled eggs," Polly said. "Wanda made them."

"Don't mind if I do." Gus helped himself to a fat egg.

"Hey," Wanda scolded as Ed returned. "Those are for the picnic."

"Dad and I have been busting our chops out there, sweets. We need sustenance."

He'd dubbed her with the nickname after discovering the true depths of her sugar craving.

He popped the whole egg into his mouth and polished it off with relish. "You did good."

"They're excellent," Ed agreed, eating his in several bites.

"You've been holding out on me, woman." Gus gave Wanda's hair a playful tug.

As always, his teasing grin was impossible to resist. He swept her back over his arm, making her giggle. But the heat flashing in his eyes wiped the smile from her face. When his lips touched hers the world faded away. She wrapped her arms around his neck and returned the kiss.

"Get a load of them," Ed said.

"Cool down, you two, or you'll give me heart palpitations," Polly quipped.

Wanda batted Gus away and straightened. Cheeks hot, she smoothed her summer blouse and cleared her throat.

Polly laughed. "You two remind me of myself and Martin." She wore the wistful look that crossed her face whenever she mentioned her husband. "We couldn't keep our hands off each other, either, both before and after we married. I suspect when you two wed, you'll be the same way."

"I'd say so," Ed agreed.

This wasn't the first time they'd assumed Wanda

and Gus were destined to become husband and wife. If Polly had her way, they'd get married next week.

Cindy also expected an engagement soon. Wanda had told her about Gus, but nothing specific. The less her mother knew the better. She'd seen his photo and stats on the calendar and was impressed that Wanda had "caught" the firefighter.

As if anyone could "catch" another person. Wanda was still rolling her eyes over the antiquated terminology.

"We've only been together a couple months," Gus reminded Polly and his father. "It's too soon to think about marriage."

"Way too early," Wanda agreed.

Liar. If he proposed today, she'd accept without a second thought.

Now that you've let yourself go, he'll never marry you, let alone propose, taunted a little voice in her mind that sounded a lot like her mother. In reality, Cindy had no idea Wanda had traded her flamboyance for a tamer look that felt more like her true self.

Doubts flooded back. Wanda fingered her brown hair—the natural color. Mostly. She'd added blonde highlights but nothing dramatic. Soon after she and Gus had officially entered a relationship, she'd tossed her supply of vivid highlight colors and had washed the non-permanent dye from her hair. No more contact lenses or bright lipsticks, either.

After two months, she'd grown comfortable with her toned-down self. Gus wasn't the only one who liked the more natural look. Ed called her a beautiful young woman, and a whole host of people had complimented her. Yet at the moment, Wanda questioned the wisdom of easing up on the makeup.

As if sensing her need for reassurance, Gus gave

her the same tender, intimate smile he'd shone on her this morning, after they'd made love. She was still glowing from the soft kisses that had awakened her and quickly ignited into passionate sex.

Her own smile bloomed. They were together and happy. That mattered more than words of love or a marriage proposal.

Refusing to waste one more second of this glorious day on silly insecurities, she pushed them away.

Ed went home to shower and take care of his own yard before returning to spend the evening with Polly.

"I could use a shower, too," Gus said. "Okay if I use the upstairs bathroom, Aunt Polly?"

"As long as you clean up after yourself. You know I can't get up there anymore."

While Gus was upstairs, Wanda joined Polly at the table and helped wrap the eggs per the woman's instructions, twisting the ends of the wax paper around each egg. "I wish you and Ed would come with us to Guff's Lake for the picnic and fireworks," she said. "Adam, Sam, Rafe and Jillian would love for you to join us. So would little William."

Polly waved off the suggestion. "I've been to more picnics and firework displays than you and Gus combined. Besides, it's hot outside. I'm more comfortable here, where it's nice and cool. So is Ed. He'll be back in time for dinner. Later we'll watch the festivities on TV. Leave us some fried chicken, a couple carrot sticks and two deviled eggs, and we'll be fine."

"But dinner is hours away. I hate to leave you alone on a holiday."

Polly's lips thinned. "If this is another attempt to convince me to move into a retirement community where I'll be surrounded by other people, save your breath. I am not leaving this house!"

Where had that come from? Wanda's eyes widened. "I wasn't even thinking about that."

"See that you don't. I'm perfectly capable of looking after myself."

When Gus returned, his hair was wet and he'd changed into a clean T-shirt, cargo shorts and sandals. "Ready to go?" he asked.

"As soon as we fill the cooler."

After packing ice, pop and the food into the cooler, Gus kissed Polly's weathered cheek. "I'll call you tomorrow."

"You and Ed have fun tonight." Wanda leaned down and hugged Polly's shoulders. She wasn't a thin woman, but her shoulders felt bony and frail.

Wanda hated that, but Polly didn't want her sympathy or concern.

She and Gus headed out.

~

IN THE AREA adjacent to Guff's Lake Resort, the Fourth of July picnic began to wind down. Seated on a blanket on the grass, belly full to bursting, Gus gave Sam a thumbs-up. "Best cherry pie ever."

Beside him, Wanda gave an enthusiastic nod. "You could make a mint selling these."

"Haven't I been telling you, babe?" Adam said.

"Only every time I bake us a pie." Sam smiled. "When I open my own bakery next year and don't have to spend as much time delivering baked goods all over town, I plan to offer several different kinds of pies."

"Including chocolate?" Wanda asked, her expressive eyes so hopeful Gus chuckled.

"Definitely," Sam replied.

"I can't wait. I'm going to bring them in for birthdays at the salon. By then, it'll be all mine."

"Super idea," Jillian said. "I'd like to do that for my pottery students, but I don't think working with clay and eating pie are a good fit."

The women launched a discussion of the ups and downs of running a small business. Moments later, they headed for the bathroom with Sam's cute kid, William.

Rafe and Jillian had arrived hours earlier and staked out a shady spot with a first-rate view of the upcoming fireworks.

After a scorching day, the setting sun and light breeze rustling through the trees had cooled the air to bearable.

Gus stretched out his legs, rested on his elbows and glanced around. Families and friends of all ages had gathered for the festivities. He recognized many familiar faces, some he even knew by name.

He was sitting up when Wanda and the others returned. She sat down between his splayed legs. Automatically, his arms went around her. He rested his chin on her head. The scents of lavender and woman filled his nostrils.

"Mm," she murmured, snuggling closer.

The familiar hunger rose up, along with a certain part of his anatomy. Unbelievable as it seemed, he wanted her more every day.

They got along great. He looked forward to their lively conversations and easy laughter. Things were going well. He should have been content. But recently, the restless, penned-in feeling he knew so well had reared up, dogging him at the most unexpected times.

Like now.

Wanda never pressured him about their relationship and the future. Hell, she was as wary as he was. So what was his problem?

She glanced over her shoulder at him. "You're all tense."

"Hazards of the job." That was no lie. "I may not be on duty tonight, but you can bet I'm keeping an eye out for smoke and flames. So are Adam and Rafe."

His buds nodded. The Fourth of July with all its festivities was notorious for unwanted fires and injuries.

Rafe murmured something to Jillian that brought pink to her cheeks. They shared a long look. "We need a walk," he announced. "We'll be back." Holding hands, they wandered off.

Adam and Sam dug boxes of snakes and sparklers from their basket and handed them to William, who danced with excitement.

Wanda wriggled against Gus's hard-on and his restlessness faded. "Two can play this game," he growled, nuzzling her neck.

She half turned, so he could kiss her.

"Look, Mom, they're kissing like you and Adam!"

William's horrified expression made them all smile. Adam ruffled his hair. "That's okay, sport. They like each other. Let's go to the safe area and light those sparklers before the big fireworks."

The happy trio headed off.

Alone with Wanda, Gus ran his hands up and down her bare arms. "Quarter for your thoughts."

"It's Polly. When I invited her to come with us this afternoon, she accused me of trying to talk her into moving into a retirement community. I wasn't, Gus."

"She has been more irritable than usual," he agreed. "Maybe she's beginning to realize we're right about the move."

"That's not how she sounded today. What are we going to do about her, Gus?"

For all his misgivings about him and Wanda, Gus appreciated her concern and willingness to be involved in the situation, as well as the time she spent time with his great aunt. "I still don't know, and I don't want to think about it today."

He tipped his chin upward, where dusk colored the sky in brilliant pinks and oranges. "Get a load of the sunset."

"Gorgeous." Resting her head against his chest, she let out a contented sigh. "This is about the best Fourth of July I can ever remember. It sure tops a regular Saturday night date."

"It's pretty special."

Long minutes of comfortable silence passed before Adam, Sam and William returned. The boy was full of stories about the sparklers and the other kids he'd met.

"I wonder what happened to Rafe and Jillian?" Wanda said.

Remembering the private look between them, Gus had a fair idea. "They'll be here before it gets dark."

He was mistaken. By the time they returned, darkness had already fallen. In the haloes of the safety lights sprinkled around the grounds, he noted Jillian's mussed hair and the relaxed expressions on her and Rafe's faces.

He didn't have to be a rocket scientist to figure out what they'd been up to, but then, every guy in town knew about the hideaways around the lake where lovers could be alone. With most of the crowd congregated near the fireworks display area, privacy elsewhere in the resort area was a sure bet.

Gus contemplated stealing away with Wanda, but

then the first fireworks exploded in the sky. She made a sound of sheer pleasure, matched only by William's delighted laughter.

As the display continued and the night air cooled, she rested her full body weight against him and laid her hands sweetly on his thighs. Gus was used to towering over women when on his feet. Even seated, he dominated Wanda. She was tiny. Not petite—too many curves—but small enough that he felt protective. She'd probably smack him if she knew. Smiling to himself, he hugged her close.

She kissed his forearm. Tenderness washed over him.

Mine.

She pointed at the sky, then clapped with unfettered glee. He'd never seen her let loose this way, felt awed to witness such joy.

Moments later, his awe faded into the old uneasiness that left him unsettled. During the last cascade of fireworks, he finally pinned a label to it.

He was freaking sacred and unsure which rattled him more—the fullness in his chest or the need to shake free of it.

23

After the fireworks, Wanda helped Gus gather their belongings. Along with their friends, they joined the throng of weary celebrators migrating toward the Guff's Lake Resort parking area. Sometime later, tired but content, she sank into the Jeep's passenger seat.

Gus's vehicle and the cavalcade of other cars idled in line, waiting to exit. Gus was silent and solemn.

"Worn out?" she asked, rolling her head toward him.

"Dead. It's been a long day."

"If you would just sleep in..." she teased.

She hoped for a smile, but he remained somber. The apprehension that had nagged at her this morning threatened to return. Tonight had been wonderful, and she would not ruin it with doubts. Besides, Gus had been so attentive and loving tonight. Poor guy was exhausted, that was all.

"Mind you, I'm not complaining," she added, fighting the tight feeling in her stomach. "I happen to like the way you wake me early in the morning."

"Yeah? Me, too."

At last he grinned. Limp with relief, she made herself comfortable.

"How about some music?" He turned on the radio.

An oldie instrumental filled the car. They were still in the lot, edging toward the exit, when Wanda's eyes drifted shut.

The next thing she knew, Gus was gently nudging her awake. "You're home."

Rubbing her eyes and stretching, she slung her purse over her shoulder and slid out of the car.

Upstairs in her apartment, Gus yawned. "I can't wait to crash."

As soon as they climbed into bed, he kissed her forehead. "Night, sweets."

He rolled onto his side, facing away from her.

Every bit as exhausted, she was in no mood for sex and hadn't expected it. But turning away? That was new.

Wanda shivered. She fell asleep hugging her pillow and wondering what had changed since they'd left the resort.

Sometime later, Gus woke her with a kiss every bit as dazzling as the fireworks. He made love with her, as passionate and giving as she could ever want.

"How do you do it?" he asked in the afterglow that followed.

As sated and drowsy as she was, she struggled to speak. "Do what?"

"Rock my world every time." From behind, he wrapped himself around her, spoon-style.

As usual, she'd worried for nothing. Feeling ridiculous and ready to fall back to sleep—it was two o'clock in the morning—she snuggled close.

Gus nuzzled the crook of her shoulder. "Your skin

is so soft and smooth, and you always smell so good. Holding you is a gift."

Her heart overflowed with love. So much love that the words spilled out before she could swallow them back. "I love you, Gus."

In the darkness, facing away from him, she couldn't see his face, but she felt him freeze. He didn't comment, didn't say he loved her.

Wanda bit her lip so hard, she broke the skin. And cursed herself for her lapse. As she'd feared all along, blurting out her feelings was a colossal mistake.

TOO STUNNED TO DO OTHERWISE, Gus continued to cocoon Wanda. His mind spun. She loved him.

He didn't know what to do with that, what to say.

Never mind that he had feelings for her, too. Strong ones that confused him and urged him to bolt.

She'd gone tense and absolutely still, as if holding her breath in fear.

Join the crowd.

He still didn't move. Couldn't, until the moment passed.

Eventually, she relaxed and her breathing evened out. Gus wished he could fall back asleep as easily. Instead, he was wide awake and all jumbled up inside.

He knew what he had to do. End the relationship. Knowing he would break her heart killed him.

Gus silently slung every bad name he could think of at himself, but it didn't change anything. He would have to tell her, the sooner the better.

At four a.m., needing to go home and figure out how to do that, he carefully slipped out of bed.

She was such a heavy sleeper, he didn't expect her

to stir. She surprised him, levering herself up on one arm and squinting at him.

"Where are you going?" she asked.

"Can't sleep. I'm behind on the mapping part of the inspection project. I need to put in some serious hours on that and clear a couple other things off my plate. Stay in bed. I'll let myself out."

Her forehead creased, and he braced for questions he wasn't prepared to answer.

To his relief, she nodded. "Okay."

She dropped back onto her pillow and closed her eyes.

Without a backward glance, he padded silently from the bedroom.

24

Waking up without Gus Sunday morning felt strange. Lonely. Not that they spent every night together. But the Fourth had been so special, and the middle-of-the-night sex so tender and amazing, Wanda had assumed he would stay through breakfast.

Then she'd told him she loved him.

"Why did I do that?" she moaned, smacking her forehead.

She needed to talk to Nadia and Rochelle. Unfortunately, both were both out of town, Rochelle camping in the Siskiyous with Matt for a week, and Nadia visiting her parents in Portland through Monday.

There was only one thing to do—keep busy. Wanda spent the day in a flurry of cleaning, laundry and other chores. She ironed dresses and blouses, then went out to browse the sale rack at her favorite dress store. A skirt or top would make her feel better. But nothing interested her, and she left empty-handed. Next, she bought groceries.

After returning home, she put the food away. Although she knew her savings account balance to the penny, she double checked it and then updated her budget. As yet, she didn't quite have what she needed for the down payment on Tommie's, but with judicious spending and a few more wedding gigs, she would soon have more than enough. That at least was good news.

For dinner, she pulled out the brownies she'd bought at the grocery. The evening was too warm to sit on the balcony, so she plunked on the living room couch and tuned into a *Gilmore Girls* marathon. The TV series that had ended years ago remained one of her all-time favorites and would provide a much-needed distraction. She ate straight from the pan, mixing brownies with a pint of vanilla ice cream.

If Gus had been around, he'd have shaken his head and teased her for overdosing on chocolate and sugar. But if he'd been here, she wouldn't be pigging out.

During a commercial break, she received a text from him.

Crazy day. Made solid progress on the mapping & looked at a '64 Mustang in bad shape. Talk later.

No miss you, sweets, or any of the warm, suggestive endearments she'd come to expect. Last night's confession had put a definite damper on their relationship. Maybe even killed it.

Dear God, what if he broke up with her? Wanda didn't know if she could bear that.

Not about to reveal her insecurities, she kept her reply light and upbeat. *Busy here, too. Cool about the Mustang!*

She watched five seasons of the *Gilmore Girls* marathon, laughing and crying and bingeing, before she hit the remote's off button. Not a brownie crumb or a single drop of melting vanilla ice cream remained. Sometimes, a girl did what she needed to.

Around midnight, dazed from TV overload and sick to her stomach from way too much sugar and chocolate, she staggered to the bathroom and got ready for bed.

Drained and craving sleep, she slid between freshly laundered sheets, sighed and closed her eyes. Instead of falling instantly into la-la land, she tossed and turned for what seemed hours, chastising herself for letting her feelings out and wishing she could turn back the clock.

But that never worked. At last, lying on Gus's side of the bed and using his pillow, she slept.

~

BADLY IN NEED OF ADVICE, Wanda contacted Jillian and Sam shortly after she woke up Monday morning. She considered them friends, and both had known Gus longer than she had.

They met for lunch at The Rogue, on the opposite side of town from the Guff's Lake Fire Department. Too far away for Gus, Adam, Rafe or any of their crewmates to stop by on a work day.

Jillian and Sam had already found a booth. Wanda slid into the bench facing the two women.

After the usual chitchat and a visit from the waitress, Wanda cleared her throat. "I need your take on something, but you can't tell Adam or Rafe."

Sam's lips twitched. "What happens at The Rogue—"

"Stays at The Rogue," Jillian finished.

Reassured, Wanda jumped straight to the bottom line. "I don't think Gus wants to be with me anymore."

Saying the words out loud hurt.

"You mean he broke up with you?" Jillian's face

filled with sympathy. "You two seemed so happy at the fireworks."

"It was a wonderful evening," Wanda agreed. "We haven't broken up yet, but we will."

"Did something happen?" Sam asked.

"He left in the middle of the night. He's never done that before."

Their food arrived.

"His aunt isn't in great shape," Jillian commented when the waitress left. "Maybe she was in trouble and he had to go."

"He didn't mention her then or when he texted last night. He said he couldn't sleep and had things to do."

"Which could be the truth. And he did text you."

Jillian nodded. "He doesn't strike me as a guy who'd walk away from a relationship without a word."

"He'd never do that," Wanda agreed. "But it's only a matter of time." Unable to eat, she toyed with her sandwich.

Sam frowned. "I'm glad you called. You need us to talk you down from that cliff you're standing on."

"You haven't heard the whole story. I did something really stupid. I told Gus I love him. That's when he started acting weird. Me and my big mouth." Hugging herself did nothing to ease the ache in her heart.

"Newsflash—your feelings for him have been obvious for a long time," Sam pointed out.

"Maybe to you. I don't think he knew until I spelled it out."

"His feelings for you are equally clear. He cares."

"A lot," Jillian said. "Some guys tend to be closed-up emotionally. Gus may not realize how deep his feelings run, or he could be afraid of love. Rafe was. When we first started seeing each other, he was super wary of getting involved. I got tired of that and left him alone, and he finally came around."

"I could share similar stories about Adam." Sam reached across the table and squeezed Wanda's hand. "Don't give up. Talk to him."

"What would I say—excuse me for admitting I love you?" Wanda shook her head. "He'd think I was chasing after him, and I refuse to do that." Ever again.

"If he loves you and he's anything like Rafe, you won't have to," Jillian said. "Keep busy and go about your business. You'll see."

"That's the thing. He doesn't love me. Oh, he likes me a lot, but that's based on lust." A lust no-doubt dampened to extinction by her lapse in judgment. "I know him. Baring my feelings made him feel pressured. He really hates that."

She wouldn't be in this situation if she hadn't convinced herself they had a future together when she knew better. A huge mistake. "If he's tired of me, well, I've been hurt before. I'll survive."

She always did. Even if her love for Gus dwarfed the feelings for any other man she'd been with.

"Don't jump off that cliff just yet," Jillian said. "It's been less than forty-eight hours. If it were me, I'd talk to Gus. A conversation isn't the same as chasing after him."

Make him even more claustrophobic? Wanda went cold at very idea. Years of experience had taught her sharing concerns about the relationship caused no end of conflict and fighting, made things worse. "I'm not good at bringing up problems, not with a guy I'm seeing."

"If you want a real relationship, you have to talk," Jillian insisted.

"My sentiments exactly." Sam glanced at her watch.

"I hate to leave, but I need to pick up William from his play date."

They parted company with hugs and Wanda's promise to keep them posted.

On the drive home, she thought about what they'd said. That brought up ugly memories. How many times had she and Crystal covered their ears and cowered in their bedroom, while Cindy and her boyfriend of the month screamed and argued? The fights usually occurred when one wanted more than the other cared to give.

Wanda had suffered through a milder variation of the same thing when she'd confronted Wayne near the end of their relationship.

Why would hashing out her issues with Gus be any different? Shuddering at the very thought of fighting with him, she dismissed her friends' advice.

Anyway, she already knew the crux of the problem. Gus wanted her body—at least he had—but not her love.

As much as that hurt, there was no one to blame but herself. He'd treated her well and she'd tossed out her plan and rolled over like a puppy craving a belly rub.

Now she would pay the price.

Would she never learn?

25

On Monday, Gus and his team put out a nasty fire at a sporting goods store, caused by faulty wiring. They didn't return to the station until lunchtime.

"With the weather so dry, it's going to be a busy month," Captain Comings commented during the meal.

His thoughts on Wanda, Gus only half-listened. He dreaded hurting her. He also worried about Aunt Polly.

At last night's Sunday dinner she'd asked why Wanda hadn't joined them. Gus's explanation that he'd worked all day and she had things to do had failed to satisfy her. She knew him too well for—

"Gus?" Owen jabbed him hard.

"Huh?" he grumbled.

"The captain asked you a question."

Gus turned to Captain Comings with raised eyebrows. "Yes?"

"I asked for your ETA on the safety inspection project."

"I said I'd get it to you in early August, and I will." To Gus's own ears he sounded testy.

The captain narrowed his eyes. "Is there a problem?"

Yeah. He was all torn up about Wanda. "No, sir. Just a lot on my mind."

During the remainder of the meal the crew left him alone.

In the apparatus bay later, Gus did his part to ready the fire engine he was assigned to for the next call. That done, he laid out his protective clothing and shoes.

Owen did the same. "What kind of stuff do you have on your mind?"

"None of your damn business."

"What put the burr up your ass?"

The rest of the crew wandered over. Nosey jokers.

After rolling his eyes, Gus shrugged. They'd know soon enough. "Ever felt trapped?"

"Here?" Owen asked.

"Hell, no. I enjoy what I do. Trapped by a woman."

"Not if I can help it," Max quipped.

A couple guys laughed, but Owen understood. "Oh, man, don't tell me you're walking away from Wanda."

"She's great," Rafe said. "Perfect for you."

"I don't know. I feel..." Gus paused and searched for a way to describe his emotions. "Things changed."

"What'd she do, man, ask for a commitment?" Max asked.

"You could say that. She used the L word."

Owen nodded. "You've always had issues with that."

True. Gus had never understood why. All he knew was, as soon Wanda said she loved him, his gut had tensed and his head had screamed at him to get out while he still could.

"You're gonna break up with her," Adam said.

Gus blew out a weighty sigh. "I don't want to hurt her, but—"

"Then don't. Wanda's terrific."

"Yeah, but—"

Over the shrilling intercom, Sarah McCone, the chief dispatcher, announced a fire.

In seconds, Gus and his crewmates dressed and climbed aboard their vehicles.

Max pushed a button, raising the two large apparatus bay doors, and Liam, the engineer, aka driver, started the siren and hotfooted out the door. An aid car and the second fire engine followed.

Adrenaline pumping, Gus buckled into his seat. "Where are we headed?"

"The west side of town." Liam shared the address.

Gus felt sick. "That's Aunt Polly's house."

~

WITHIN MINUTES of arriving at Aunt Polly's, the fire, which had started in the kitchen, was contained and extinguished. Unfortunately, Aunt Polly hadn't called it in as quickly as she should have. At least she'd managed to make her way outside, away from the smoke and flames.

Rob and Daniel, two of the crew pulling paramedic duty this month, examined her. To Gus's relief, they pronounced her shaken but otherwise unharmed.

Rob kept her company on the porch, while Gus and Owen tromped through the main floor with an infrared device to check for undetected heat inside the walls, an indicator the fire had spread. Max checked for the presence of toxic chemicals. They repeated the tests in the basement and upstairs.

To Gus's relief, they found no traces of either outside the kitchen. Unfortunately, the entire main floor reeked of smoke and the nasty charred smell that often accompanied a structural fire.

When Gus joined Aunt Polly on the porch, Rob nodded and left them alone.

"Why don't you sit down?" she invited from her favorite redwood rocking chair.

"I don't want to get your nice patio cushions dirty." Gus squatted down to eye level. "How are you doing?"

"I'm embarrassed, of course. What a foolish old woman I've become. I'm worried about the kitchen. Even out here, I can smell it." She made a face.

"Once we made sure the fire was out, we opened all the windows in the house," Gus explained. "Do you want to walk through?"

"No." She gave him an anxious look. "Tell me about the damage, and don't sugar-coat a thing."

She always had preferred her information straight-up and clean. Gus gave her what she asked for. "First, the good news. The basement is fine, and except for a slight smoky smell, the upstairs is okay. The main floor, not so much. The entire wall behind the stove will need to be replaced, along with the floor and those curtains you like so much."

She'd gone pale. "What else needs to be done?"

"That smoke smell is hard to get rid of. I'd have the whole house scrubbed and repainted by odor removal experts. You may end up replacing or recovering the furniture and getting new carpeting."

"Not my oriental rug."

"A thorough cleaning might work. Might not."

"Dear Lord." Aunt Polly covered her mouth with her hand.

"Hey, it's all repairable or replaceable," Gus assured her. "Your homeowners insurance should cover some of the cost. Our benefit fund will help, too. I'll pick up the rest."

"I can't let you do that."

"Sure you can. I make a bundle on those classic car restorations, I can afford it."

"But this isn't your—"

"Do me a favor, and for once, accept help from your family."

"I don't like it but all right." She sighed. "Where am I supposed to live during all these repairs?"

"If my place was bigger, you could stay with me. We're lucky Dad has the day off today. I spoke with him, and he's on his way over to pick you up. He's going to put a bed in his den for you."

"A person can hardly turn around in that den." Aunt Polly worked the collar of her blouse between her arthritic fingers. "Maybe Wanda has room for me."

"She would if she could," Gus said. "But her apartment isn't much bigger than mine." He hated the anxious expression on his great aunt's face. "I'll do my best to find you a more comfortable place to stay. Until then, Dad's den will have to do. We'll make it work. Do you want me to call your insurance agent before I leave?"

He expected her to insist on taking care of the matter herself. To his surprise, she gave a meek nod.

"If you wouldn't mind. I feel so foolish," she repeated, pushing the rocker slowly.

She was more rattled than Gus had realized. So was he. Over the years he'd battled a fair share of fires, but this one hit a little too close to home. "You scared the spit out of me this afternoon," he admitted.

"Scared myself, too." She chafed her arms with hands that trembled from more than age.

"Tell me what happened."

"Well, I slept late and woke up feeling energetic enough to cook breakfast. Remember how I used to whip up eggs, bacon and toast on Saturday mornings?"

Gus licked his lips. "Best breakfast ever."

He'd served the same meal to Wanda after their first night together. Before things had become complicated. That morning seemed a lifetime ago.

She would want to know about the fire.

"I made the bacon first," Aunt Polly said. "You know how greasy it is. I was laying the fried strips on paper towels when Mother Nature called. At my age, that means now. In my haste to get to the bathroom, I forgot to turn off the gas burner." She looked sheepish. "The paper towels must have been too close to the flames. They caught fire, and by the time I returned to the kitchen the flames had spread. It could happen to anyone, right? I never did get anything to eat."

She attempted a smile. Gus did not. "We'll get you fed pronto. Dad will take you out."

He took hold of her blue-veined hands. "This is one reason I don't want you living alone anymore, Aunt Polly," he said gently. "You need to be at a place that serves you meals in a dining room, or if you decide to cook in your apartment, staff members can reach you in time to prevent fire damage like this."

Instead of arguing, she considered his words. Definite progress. He was on the verge of suggesting they look at retirement communities after his shift ended Wednesday, when his father pulled up.

Gus updated him and then kissed Aunt Polly's wrinkled cheek. "The crew is waiting. I need to get back to the station. I'll call you at Dad's tonight."

26

Having left The Rogue without dessert, Wanda drove to the nearest drugstore for a candy bar. On the way, she considered Gus and her options. Was it best to wait for him to break up with her or salvage her pride and break up with him first?

Her usual way was to hang on tight and do whatever she could to save the relationship. Which never worked and left her pride in tatters.

The second route, then. And yet...a tiny part of her clung to the hope that Sam and Jillian were right, that Gus loved her but didn't realize it.

In that case, Wanda didn't want to break things off. At the same time, she refused to sit around, twiddling her thumbs, while he figured it out.

What do to, what to do? Deep in thought, she stopped for a red light.

How could Gus or any man love you? Cindy's voice chided in her mind. *You're not worth—*

"Stop it!" Wanda demanded.

The woman in a VW Bug the next lane over gave her an odd look.

Feeling silly for talking to herself out loud with the

car windows down, Wanda pinned her gaze on the light until it turned green.

Still in a quandary about what to do, she headed forward on automatic pilot and considered resurrecting her plan. Joining a monastery might work out better.

As she pulled into the drugstore lot, her Bluetooth lit up. "Gus Viggio," the speaker announced in its smooth female voice.

He'd better not break up with her over the phone. Her heart squeezed and her temper ratcheted up a notch or three. Needing chocolate and fast, she considered ignoring the call.

But he never phoned from work in the middle of the day. It had to be an emergency.

Worried and forgetting her annoyance with him, she slid into a parking space. "Hi. What's wrong?"

"First, Aunt Polly is okay."

Her shoulders relaxed a fraction. Before she could say, "Phew," he exhaled loudly.

"I just came from her place. There was a fire."

"Oh, no." Horrified, Wanda slumped in her seat. "You said she's okay."

"Rob and Daniel examined her and she is."

"That's good. Tell me how the fire started."

"She left a burner on, and a couple paper towels caught fire. The kitchen is a mess, and the main floor sustained smoke damage. The upstairs, too. The basement is okay. She has to move out for a while."

"She could have burned down the whole house. And herself." Wanda shuddered at the thought.

"Yeah." Gus cleared his throat as if fighting hard-core emotion.

He'd never sounded so spooked. Wanda wished he

were in the car with her so she could wrap her arms around him. Although he might not want that.

"She must be upset," she said, feeling awful herself. "Where will she sleep tonight? You don't have room. I could give her my bed and sleep on the living room couch."

"I appreciate the offer, but you don't want to do that. The repairs could take months. She made plans to stay with my dad. He picked her up a little while ago."

"Do you think she'll be more open to moving now?"

"I touched on the idea, but we didn't get a chance to talk much. Dad promised to mention it again. I will, too."

"I'm going to call her, Gus, and let her know I'm thinking of her."

"You don't have to do that."

"You'd rather I didn't," Wanda guessed, trying to sound nonchalant instead of confused and hurt.

What had Sam said at lunch? *If you want a real relationship, you have to talk.*

Wanda wanted to know what was up—so bad, she almost swallowed her fear of conflict and asked. Almost.

She didn't. Gus had enough on his plate. She wasn't about to pile on more.

"Feel free to contact her," he said. "But wait a few hours. She hasn't eaten today, and Dad took her out. Then she'll need to get settled at his place and probably take a nap."

"Of course. What can I do to help?"

"Nothing I can think of. Hang on." She heard Gus cover the phone and speak to someone before he came back. "Lots of stuff going on today. Gotta run."

"Thanks for letting me know, Gus."

"Sure. Talk to you later."

Five minutes after leaving the drugstore, Wanda finished her chocolate bar. And thought about Polly. Poor woman. Surely after what had happened today, she would change her mind about retirement communities.

For her sake, Wanda hoped so.

"I DON'T LIKE STAYING at your dad's," Aunt Polly sniffed when Gus drove her to her hair appointment Wednesday. "His apartment is cramped, and he fusses over me like a mother hen. You promised to find me a different place to stay."

Gus had checked with everyone he could think of, but no one had room to board a seventy-nine-year-old woman for several months. "I'll keep looking," he assured her. She seemed especially tired this morning. "Sure you're up for a hair appointment?"

"Knowing I'll see Wanda is the reason I got out of bed this morning. That and Ed's lumpy hide-a-bed mattress. Wanda has been just darling, calling both Monday and Tuesday nights. I adore the girl, and I can't wait until you make her a real member of our family."

Gus shifted in his seat. "As I keep saying, it's too soon."

Especially when it wasn't going to happen. His great aunt had no idea he planned to break things off with Wanda. She was already upset enough about her house. He hadn't even talked with Wanda yet.

Thanks to work, he hadn't seen her and wasn't about to do it over the phone. As painful as it might be, the conversation needed to happen in person, and soon.

He escorted Aunt Polly into Tommie's. Wanda was waiting. In a soft pink above-the-knee, sleeveless summer shift and strappy heels, she looked cool and beautiful. She barely spared him a glance before she opened her arms to Aunt Polly.

"I'm so glad to see you!" she exclaimed, sounding close to tears. "How are you doing?"

"I'm managing, but I'd be better if Gus found me a nice place to stay while I wait out the repairs on my house. As much as I love Ed, he drives me crazy. You should see the clutter at his place!" She wrinkled her nose. "Gus, will you get me a cup of decaf? I'm going to head over to Wanda's station and sit down."

"Go on ahead, Polly," Wanda said. "I'll get the coffee and be with you shortly."

She accompanied Gus to the coffee pot. He caught a whiff of her hair, inhaled appreciatively and started to grab her hand. Then caught himself. From now on, touching her was off-limits.

"On the phone last night, Polly told me twice how eager she is to return to the house." Wanda shook her head. "I didn't know what to say."

"Yesterday when I brought up the subject of moving, she tore my head off."

"Thanks for the warning." Looking thoughtful, she tapped her finger to her lips. "I was talking with a client earlier, and—"

"Hey, Gus." Wanda's friend, Nadia, flashed a smile and joined them. "Excuse me, Wanda, but Polly asked me to come over here and tell you to, and I quote, 'rub noses with Gus' some other time."

"I'll tell you later," Wanda said, not quite meeting

his eyes. "Are you going to sit with us while I style her hair?"

Gus had no intention of listening to his great aunt's blatant hints about marriage. He shook his head. "I need to make calls about the house."

When he returned, his great aunt was in the bathroom again.

"Here's what I started to tell you," Wanda said. "According to one of my customers, some retirement communities offer a low-cost trial visit, where a person can stay in a furnished apartment for up to a month to get a taste of living in the community. Here's the address of the website that has the information." She handed Gus a slip of paper.

She'd found what could be the perfect solution. Grateful, Gus pocketed the information. "Sounds good. I hope Aunt Polly agrees."

"Why wouldn't she? It's temporary and cheap, and she doesn't have many other options. If she doesn't like it, she can go back to your dad's."

"Keep your fingers crossed. Look, we need to talk," Gus said, feeling like a jerk for what he had to do. "What's a good time?"

A resigned look crossed her face, disappearing so fast he wondered if he'd imagined it.

"As a matter of fact, I was about to suggest the same thing. How about tonight around seven?"

27

Ⅰn her gut, Wanda knew Gus planned to end the relationship tonight. Well, she had a surprise in store—to break-up with him instead.

She would not plead for a second chance or use sex to lure him back, even if he was the love of her life. For the first time ever, she intended to walk away with her head high and her pride intact. That at least would feel good.

At seven sharp, the security alarm downstairs beeped. He'd arrived. Determined to stay strong, she buzzed him up.

Shoulders squared, she poised for his knock. Then made him wait a minute while she stuffed the hurt and anger deep inside, where he would never see. She let him in.

"Hey." His terse nod mirrored her own tension.

In the living room, she gestured for him to sit, then took the chair across from the coffee table.

"I've been thinking about us..." she began.

"Me, too. You wouldn't believe the stuff I need to take care of since the fire. Between working with the insurance agent, lining up estimates for the repairs and trying to find a comfortable place for Aunt Polly to stay, I barely have time to eat. And don't forget the Mustang I'm supposed to restore. Dad is working just as hard, driving a bus forty hours a week and spending all his free time taking care of Aunt Polly. We're both stretched thin."

He did sound busy. Could she be mistaken? Maybe Gus didn't want to break up, simply needed her help. Melting a little and eager to do whatever she could, she leaned forward. "If you're asking me to take on some of your burdens, I—"

"I'm not." Gus cleared his throat and scrubbed his hand over his face, and her heart stuttered. "I'm snowed under here. I think we need a time out."

She'd expected this since the night her feelings had slipped out. Had bolstered herself with her plan to leave first and salvage her pride. Still, her heart ripped in two.

Do not cry. Do not. Hiding her pain, she forced a neutral expression. "Funny, I was about to break up with you."

He did a double take. "I thought... You said..."

"That I love you? Look where that got me." To her horror, her eyes filled.

"Don't cry." He stood and moved to put his arms around her.

"Stay away," she ordered, blinking hard. "I am not crying."

With a heavy sigh, he sank back down. "I never wanted to hurt you."

"I can't say you didn't warn me." From a well of strength Wanda didn't realize she possessed, she summoned a bright smile. "My love for you made you claustrophobic."

This time, she rose. She opened the door and

stepped aside, giving Gus as wide a berth as possible in the small entry.

"Don't you want talk about this?" he asked.

What she wanted was to hang onto her dignity. "There's nothing to say except good-bye."

He raised his hand as if to touch her, but at her dirty look, his arm fell to his side. "Take care."

She barely shut the door behind him before she fell apart.

SOME THIRTY MINUTES after Wanda's heart split open, at the tail end of a long, messy cry, her cell phone rang.

Polly Becker, the screen said. Wouldn't you know.

She didn't feel like picking up, but she couldn't ignore a call from the woman.

"I haven't heard from this evening," Polly said. "I was starting to worry."

"Oh." Wanda sniffled. "Was I supposed to phone you?"

"We spoke the last two nights, and I expected we'd talk again tonight. I suppose since you cut my hair this morning..." She broke off as Wanda blew her nose. "That doesn't sound good at all. Don't tell me you're sick."

Sick at heart. Wanda felt awful all over, as if she'd been slammed with a two-by-four. "I'm not feeling well."

"I hope it isn't catching."

She couldn't bring herself to share what had happened. Not without dissolving into another round of tears. She refused to break down in front of Polly. "I'm not contagious."

"Ah, female problems. I remember being especially sensitive to smells and pollen that time of the month. Sometimes my nose ran, too."

This suffering had nothing to do with her cycle and everything to do with who she was. Being herself hadn't held Gus's interest any more than pretending to be who she wasn't had held the interest of previous boyfriends. You sure you want to hear about it?

Fresh tears gathered behind her eyes and threatened to leak out. She scrubbed them away. "I really should go."

"Put your feet up, take a pain reliever and feel better. Will I see you at Sunday dinner? I'm not sure where Gus and his dad want to eat, but it's bound to be someplace good."

Knowing she would never share another meal with Gus, Polly and Ed felt lonely and sad. She'd so hoped they'd become a real family. Wanda bit her lip. "I wish I could, but I have plans. Sleep well."

"You, too."

After disconnecting, she stared numbly at her cell phone. She thought about letting her friends know what had happened but didn't feel up to the conversation. Tonight she was stuck with her own miserable company. And chocolate.

Although she hadn't bought groceries in nearly a week, which severely limited her options, she scrounged up a half-eaten carton of fudge ripple ice cream and a bag of chocolate chips. She dumped a handful of chips and a slug of milk into a bowl, nuked and stirred until melted, and then poured the makeshift hot fudge sauce into the ice cream carton.

Spoon in hand, she headed for the balcony to sit in the darkness and drown her sorrows in sugar. Before long, the sundae disappeared. But not the emptiness inside.

Forget wishing on a shooting star or fantasizing about the family in the two-story house with all the windows. She needed to face the truth. She was alone and probably always would be.

It was time to give up on love.

Wanda didn't think she could feel any worse, but letting go of her long-held dream of love, marriage and a child or two hurt unbearably.

Shivering despite the warm evening, she pulled her knees up, wrapped her arms around her shins and contemplated the best way to survive the pain. Something that would help her move forward.

The plan that had helped her get over Larry no longer fit. She wracked her mind for a new one. Before long, she had it. From tonight on, she would live for herself.

28

On Friday morning, Gus drove Aunt Polly to look at apartments at the two retirement communities he'd contacted. Make that dragged her. At first, she'd resisted, but the lure of relocating to new temporary quarters proved too tempting to fight.

"What did you think?" he asked as he handed her into the car following the first tour.

She crossed her arms. "I wouldn't stay there for a million dollars."

"What's wrong with the place?"

"The apartment only has one bedroom, and the kitchen is awfully small."

"You don't need more than one bedroom, and you rarely cook anymore. Everything is clean and new, and the dining room on the main floor is exactly what you need."

"I won't stay here." Aunt Polly's lips thinned.

"Why am I not surprised?" he muttered, and started the Jeep. "Be that way."

"What way?"

"Your attitude sucks."

"My attitude is fine, thank you."

Gus pulled onto the road. "You complain about living with Dad and ride me to find a different place to stay. So I did, but you don't like it, either." He snorted. "If that's a good attitude, I'm a mountain climber."

"Talk about calling the kettle black! You've been in a terrible mood for days."

No lie. Breaking up sucked.

He'd been waiting for the right time to tell Aunt Polly. This seemed like it. "You're right about my lousy mood. I haven't been straight with you."

She eyed him with surprise. "Oh?"

"Wanda and I..." How to put this? "We aren't seeing each other anymore."

"Since when?"

"Wednesday night."

Aunt Polly mumbled something about finally understanding a phone call that evening and gave him a withering glare. "Why in heaven's name would you break it off with that lovely girl?"

"That's between Wanda and me."

"Pish posh." She leaned across the seat and smacked his upper arm. Hard.

"Ow!" He frowned. "What'd you do that for?"

"Because I can't reach that thick skull of yours. You're a fool, Gus."

"Thanks heaps. Look, there's Sunny Horizons." The second retirement community. He turned into the lot, found a slot in the visitors' parking area up front and braked to a stop. "I'm not talking about this with you anymore. Let's go inside."

Her damn chin lifted stubbornly. "I won't get out of the car until I have my say."

"Butt out of my love life, Aunt Polly."

As usual, she ignored him. "I swear, Augusto

Frances Viggio, you are so hardheaded, you make me look flexible."

"You couldn't be flexible if you tried."

"My point exactly. You're even worse, and let me tell you why."

He glanced at the ceiling and shook his so-called hard head. "I can't wait to hear this."

"Then be quiet and listen. You broke up with Denise after I had my stroke. You broke up with Wanda after the kitchen caught fire. I don't like being used as an excuse to end a relationship."

What the hell? Gus gaped at her. "You finally got Denise's name right. And you are not an excuse. On top of my forty-eight hours per week job with the fire department, I'm dealing with your house, the safety inspection project and a Mustang restoration. I don't have time for a relationship."

"Baloney. The other day, you told me the project was ninety-eight percent finished. You have five days a week to work on that car, and you share the burdens of the house with your dad. And for your information, I've always known Denise's name. I also know you two discussed marriage. She told me."

Gus stifled a few choice words. "You never let on."

Aunt Polly's stern expression reminded him of her years as a librarian. "Will you hush? Denise wasn't my favorite, but she loved you, and that was enough for me. When you broke off with her, I let it go, just as I have all the other girlfriends who have come and gone in your life. But this time... Your relationship with Wanda is the best thing to ever happen to you, and I won't just sit here and let you destroy it."

She shook her finger at him, as she had when he'd screwed up as a kid. "You are your own worst enemy.

Sabotaging relationships as soon you start to have deep feelings."

She didn't even pause for him to digest that, just kept going.

"Thanks to your mother, you have abandonment issues. That's understandable, but letting her despicable behavior destroy your chance for happiness is not acceptable. It's been twenty-five years—high time you moved on. Wanda is not your mother. She would never walk away from you. She's true-blue, and she loves you." Aunt Polly brushed her hands together. "I'm finished."

Reeling from the mini-psych analysis, Gus shook his head. Nothing wrong with her brain, even if she was off-base. He didn't have abandonment issues. Feeling pressured, yes, but no one liked that.

"Well?" she said.

"Since when did you become a therapist? FYI, I made peace with what my mother did a long time ago. Trust me, none of that is connected to my love life. End of subject." She opened her mouth, but he wouldn't let her speak. "You've had your say. People are waiting to show you around. Let's go."

Forty minutes into the visit, after touring the main floor and exploring the furnished apartment that was available for a thirty-day trial, she stopped giving him the cold shoulder. She sat on a chair in the sunny living room and beckoned him to join her.

"This is a comfortable chair, and the other furniture isn't half bad. I believe I could survive here for a month." She angled her chin. "Happy now?"

Gus was too torn up for that, but he was relieved. "This is good news."

"Just promise you won't leave me here until I die."

At first, he thought she was joking. A glance at her

frightened expression told him otherwise and made his chest hurt. He swallowed past the sudden lump in his throat. "You have my word on that."

They left the premises with a signed, one-month rental agreement, to begin the following day.

THE FIRST SUNDAY IN AUGUST, Gus headed to Sunny Horizons to meet Aunt Polly for brunch. Hard to believe she'd been in her temporary home three weeks.

He found her waiting for him outside the dining room, chatting animatedly with several elderly men and women.

"Here he is," she said. "This is Gus, the great nephew I told you about."

A neatly-groomed woman about Aunt Polly's age smiled and held out the firefighter calendar. "My grandson gave this to me for Christmas. Will you autograph your picture?"

"Glad to." He took care of the task and returned the calendar to her.

She beamed. "Thank you. What an exciting job you have."

The others in the group nodded.

After a few minutes of chitchat, Aunt Polly took his arm. "Let's go into the dining room and eat." She finger-waved at her friends. "I'll see you upstairs later."

"Your friends seem nice," he said.

"We play duplicate bridge together and share favorite books and magazines. They keep me on my toes."

She seemed happy, but damned if she'd move in permanently. Gus had given up pressuring her about it.

Over a surprisingly tasty brunch, he updated her on the house. "The contractor phoned yesterday. I didn't get the message until this morning."

He'd been out playing softball, the crewmates of his shift against another crew. His team had won, but they'd fought hard for the honor. After much-needed showers, both teams had met for a barbecue. Gus had done his best to enjoy the party and ignore the hole in his chest.

A hole that seemed to grow bigger instead of shrinking. He'd never hurt this bad, missed Wanda worse than he could ever remember missing anyone. The pain would pass. Had to. Moving on was best for them both.

"You and I have known for a while that the wiring is outdated," he continued. "The contractor advises us to upgrade immediately, and I agree. I don't want to worry about another fire. The plumbing isn't in great shape, either, and the roof won't make it through next winter without serious problems."

"More expensive repairs?" Her face fell.

"I'll take care of it."

"You've paid for enough. I can't let you—"

Gus held up his hand, silencing her. "We'll talk about that later. Right now, we need to discuss your living situation. You have exactly one week left of your trial month here. You can't stay in the house until the contractor finishes the repairs and the painting, which should take another month to six weeks. Longer if you add in the wiring and plumbing. You'll have to move back in with Dad."

The steely look he'd expected flashed in her eyes. "Absolutely not."

"Do you have a better solution?"

"Yes, as a matter of fact. Don't fall over, but I think I

could be happy here. Close your mouth, Gus," she scolded.

"You caught me by surprise. I never expected this."

"I never imagined I'd enjoy myself this much or make such wonderful new friends. I only wish I'd tried living here years ago." She grew solemn. "Still, I hate the idea of strangers moving into my home."

Gus thought about that. "What if I bought the place?"

Had he just offered to buy Aunt Polly's home? In dumb shock, he shut his mouth.

The look on her face was priceless. "You'd do that?"

The idea began to grow on him. He loved that house. Even after paying the contractor for work done so far, he still had plenty of money to spruce it up. "Why not?"

"What are you going to do with all that space? It's too big for one man."

She seemed to have forgotten she'd lived alone there for decades.

"Now if you and Wanda made up... She'd enjoy living in the house. Speaking of Wanda, have you thought about what I said?"

Difficult not to, but drawing a connection between his mother walking out of his life and that trapped feeling that came over him in a relationship didn't jibe. "It's been a month," Gus said. "She's probably moved on."

"She puts on a brave face, but she's pining for you."

Ditto. He'd come to dread those awkward weekly meetings. The stiff nods, pretending life was good when it sucked.

When he didn't comment, Aunt Polly made an impatient sound. "Either you didn't listen before, or your head is even harder than I thought. I suppose I have to spell it out for you. You're afraid if you feel too much, you'll get hurt, like when your mother left. That's why you do the rejecting first."

Talk about blunt. Before he could absorb the shocking accusation, Aunt Polly glanced at her watch. "I believe the front office is open for another half hour. Come with me to get an application for permanent residency. Then go home and figure out how much you can afford for the house."

29

By the following Thursday Gus had been approved for a home loan. He made an offer Aunt Polly readily accepted. In all the excitement, she didn't bring up Wanda. Neither did he.

That stuff about fear of rejection? Pure bull. He pushed the idea from his mind. Or tried. Like a boomerang, it returned, annoying the hell out of him.

As he stood at bat at the Saturday afternoon softball game, he came to grips with the harsh truth. Aunt Polly had outed his own invisible eight-hundred-pound gorilla—after all these years, his mother's desertion continued to screw with him.

Damn.

Mentally smacking himself for being so dense about something this huge, he swung at a pitch and slammed the ball over the fence, scoring an automatic home run.

Gus ran the bases anyway, at full-bore. Racing as fast as he could felt good, but he couldn't outrun the big question.

Now what?

He was mulling that over when Owen dropped a bomb in the dugout.

"According to Rafe, Jillian says Wanda's gonna hang out with a guy named Trent tomorrow afternoon," he said.

Who the hell was Trent? Wanda with another man... Gus's hands hardened into fists.

"Easy, buddy." Owen clapped him firmly on the shoulder. "Rafe said it sounds like Trent is just a friend."

Gus knew what that meant. At one time, Wanda had wanted to be his friend. They'd soon become much more.

"Bite me," he snarled.

And wished to hell Rafe was around. He and Adam had gone fishing for a few days in a place with no phone reception. Gus sure wasn't going to ask Jillian.

Owen shrugged. "You don't like that, do something about it. I happen to know she's meeting Jillian and Sam at Guff's Lake tomorrow morning for a trail walk."

Gus didn't stay for the after-game barbecue. Too much on his mind.

After a shower, he sat at the eating bar in his kitchen, nursed a beer and called himself a fool for letting Wanda go. Not because Trent had homed in on her—although he wanted to pound the guy.

Because Gus enjoyed her company, in and out of bed. Liked running things by her and making her laugh. But mostly because... He loved her.

"I'm in love with Wanda," he stated in amazement.

What do you know about that? He attempted to sit back, and almost fell off the backless barstool. Which showed how shocked he was.

Admitting the feelings he'd denied changed everything. An invisible weight he hadn't realized he carried crumbled to dust, and with it, the dark cloud that had shrouded his life since his parents had split up. Suddenly the world seemed brighter and clearer.

The one missing piece was Wanda.

Gus wanted her back. Was he too late? God above, he hoped not.

He had to find out—once he kicked his sorry past to the curb. But owning up to the old fears and shaking them off were two different things. July fourth, Wanda had claimed she loved him. Today, she could easily reject him just as his mother had.

After tossing and wrestling his demons half the night without making any headway, he fell into a fitful sleep. When he woke before dawn on Sunday, he knew one thing for sure.

Until he bared his heart to Wanda, nothing would change.

~

MID-AUGUST TEMPERATURES in Rogue Valley often climbed into the triple digits, but the early mornings tended to be pleasant. For that reason, Wanda roused herself at the ungodly hour of seven on Sunday morning. As soon as she showered, dressed and bought herself a coffee, she drove out to Guff's Lake to meet friends for a short hike.

A crowd of locals and tourists taking advantage of the as-yet mild day made for a packed parking area, and she ended up in one of the overflow lots. Not wanting to be late, she hurried to the mouth of the easy hiking loop where Rochelle, Nadia, Sam and Jillian had gathered in the shade of a sugar maple.

The women had rallied around since the breakup, offering support as only true friends can. They made a point of meeting once a week. After greeting each other, they set off.

"Good thing we started early," Wanda said, adjusting her visor hat. "It's only been a few minutes and I'm already sweating."

Rochelle nodded. "It's going be a sizzler. With the trees shading our path, we should be comfortable enough. Are you still meeting Trent this afternoon?"

Trent's fiancée, Marley, had hired Wanda to do her hair for her wedding next month. She'd introduced Wanda to Trent as "the only stylist I know with a chocolate addiction that matches mine." Wanting to surprise his bride, Trent asked Wanda to help him choose the perfect chocolates to place in their wedding suite. What a great guy.

Wanda shook her head. "He postponed until Monday."

In a clearing, she and her friends stopped to admire the stunning view of Guff's Lake. Under the brilliant sun, the clear water sparkled.

Nearby, a couple sat on a blanket under a tree, enjoying an early picnic.

"Breakfast by the lake. How romantic," Nadia sighed.

The lovers leaned across the basket between them and shared a tender kiss.

Jillian bit her lip. "I miss Rafe."

Sam nodded. "I'm sure glad he and Adam are coming home tonight."

"I left Matt in bed at my place," Rochelle said. "I hope he's still there when I get home, because suddenly I—" She slid a look at Wanda.

"Hey, it's been six weeks. I'm fine," she assured her friends.

She wasn't, but in time, she would be. Although

still struggling to let go of her longing for love and marriage, she was determined to forget Gus and be content with her friends and her own company.

Which would be a lot easier if she didn't have to face him every Wednesday. Those uncomfortable meetings left her drained.

Polly felt terrible about the breakup, but it wasn't her fault. No matter what, Wanda loved her dearly. She only wished she did a better job convincing the woman she was okay.

Her friends started a conversation about summer movies and which ones they wanted to see. From there, they segued into upcoming outdoor concerts in town.

Wanda only half-listened. No doubt, Gus was at the garage this morning, working on the Ford Mustang. He must be nearly finished by now. In a different world, she might be helping...

Quit thinking about him.

Refusing to waste another second on the man who continued to own her heart, damn him, she fell back on the one thing that kept her going. Work. Word had spread of her skills with brides-to-be, and her bookings lately included at least one wedding per weekend. Yesterday, she'd styled three generations for a wedding —the bride, her mother and her grandmother.

All had been in great spirits. Envying their close-knit relationship, but joining in the fun, Wanda had laughed along with them. The fees and the tips she'd earned had put her over the top—at last she had enough money for the down payment on Tommie's. She'd already scheduled an appointment with the loan officer at the bank. Next goal: start a budget for turning the salon into a day spa.

Career-wise, the future looked bright and secure, and she was thankful for that.

"...Never be with a man who didn't know and accept the real me," Rochelle was saying.

"The real you?" Nadia's forehead wrinkled.

"We all have quirks and secrets we only share with people we trust," Rochelle said. "The man I decide to spend my life with, and that could be Matt, had better love me, warts and all."

Wanda gave her a sideways look. "Does Matt know all your warts?"

"We've only been dating four months, so no, not everything. Those things come out little by little, usually when I'm unhappy or disagree with him. I never have been one to hold back." Rochelle grinned. "Matt claims I'm the most outspoken female he's ever known."

Nadia laughed. "He doesn't run for cover?"

"No way. He respects me for speaking up. He likes my passion, and I don't just mean the sex."

"What if he disagrees with you?" Wanda asked.

"We try to talk it through, but if we can't, we have an argument."

Sam nodded. "Adam says a good fight is a great way to clear the air and grow closer."

Wanda gaped at her. "You and Adam hit each other?"

"Of course not. We don't name call, either, go to bed mad at each other or fight in front of William. But we've had our verbal battles. When we calm down, we always feel closer."

"Same with Rafe and me." Jillian swatted at a bug. "I hate when we argue, but I sure enjoy making up."

She, Sam and Rochelle smiled at each other.

"But isn't arguing risky?" Wanda asked. "What if you break up?"

"Then you probably aren't right for each other," Sam replied.

"For me, holding in my thoughts and feelings is the worst," Rochelle said. "I get resentful, and things get ugly."

Moments later, the trail looped back to where they'd started, and the hike ended.

Sam gestured at a nearby refreshment stand that sold snacks and cold drinks. "I could use a lemonade."

"Good idea," Jillian said. "I'll grab a picnic table in the shade. Will one of you get me a cherry Slurpee?"

"I should stop at the restroom," Wanda said. "Make mine a Fudgsicle."

While she was gone, she mulled over the conversation. And realized something huge. All this time, she'd been convinced she'd shown Gus her real self.

She hadn't.

Wearing less makeup, toning down her hair and clothes, and losing the phony bubbly personality had stripped away some of the pretense. But the things that mattered most had remained hidden.

With startling insight, Wanda understood what had held her back. Blinding fear that her real self could never be enough.

Shaking, she joined her friends at the picnic table. Her cold treat was waiting.

"Something has you all worked up," Rochelle commented, looking worried.

"You can say that again. The whole time Gus and I were together, I was sure if I got along with him, we'd have a better chance of making it. Whenever I disagreed with him or wanted something he didn't, I held my tongue." Despite the rapidly rising temperature, she shivered. "We all know how that turned out. I finally understand that I cheated myself—and Gus—out of getting to know who I truly am."

Now he would never know. What a shame. Wanda sighed. "I wish I could go back and change that."

Rochelle shrugged. "Change it today."

"How?"

"Talk to him."

Could she do that? The thought both exhilarated and terrified her. "It's been six weeks. I doubt he's interested anymore."

"Don't be so sure," Jillian said. "According to Rafe, he's not dating anyone."

"Suppose I do talk to him. We broke up because I told him I loved him and he felt pressured. What's to stop him from feeling even more pressured?"

Was opening up for real worth the risk of making an even bigger fool of herself than before?

Sam touched her shoulder. "Then you're where you are now, only better because you finally spoke your truth."

With that, something inside clicked in place. Suddenly Wanda had to find Gus. Handing the unopened Fudgsicle to Nadia, she jumped up. "You're right. I have to go."

Her friends *atta-girl*'d her, and she hurried toward her car.

30

Gus pulled into the main parking lot at the Guff's Lake Resort and slowly drove around, looking for Wanda's car. She wasn't the only owner of a blue Civic. He would have to check each one.

Grumbling and on-edge to find her, he parked in the lone available space, exited the Cherokee and began his search. Before long, sweat beaded his brow, which furrowed with a healthy dose of frustration. Where in hell was her car?

She must have parked in a different lot. Or she'd already come and gone, to give herself plenty of time to get ready for that date with Trent.

At the thought, Gus growled and slid his cell phone from the hip pocket of his cargos in a white-knuckled grip. A couple headed for the lake with two young children gave him wide berth.

Focused on reaching Wanda, he paid them no mind. If things went the way he hoped, she would cancel those plans.

While her cell phone rang in his ear, he also heard her ring tone in the distance.

"Gus." She sounded taken aback.

"Where are you?" he said, glancing around.

"Hi to you, too. I'm at Guff's Lake and—"

"I know that, but where?"

"Headed for my car. How did you know?"

"Never mind. I don't see the Civic in the main lot. Where did you park?"

"The lot just south of where you are."

"Stay put." He disconnected and set off at a jog.

Moments later, he found her. Under the visor hat her face was red from the heat and a streak of dirt ran across one cheek. She'd never looked more beautiful.

His chest expanded with love. He was also nervous as hell. Shoving his hands in his pockets, he approached her. "We need to talk."

"That's funny."

He failed to see anything humorous about pouring out his heart, but at least she hadn't told him to get lost. "Cancel your date with Trent," he said.

"My date?" She frowned. "Where are you getting your information?"

"Just cancel it."

"FYI, Trent is not a date. He happens to be engaged to one of my clients, and I was supposed to help him find the right—Oh, never mind. We postponed until Monday. Why are you here?"

Owen had been right about Trent. Gus relaxed. "Are you all walked out?"

"If we keep to the shade, I could go partway around the lake."

Knowing exactly where he wanted to take her, Gus led her toward a trail.

"Aren't you curious why I made that 'funny' crack?" she said as they started up the dirt path. "By coincidence, I was about to drive to your place and talk to you."

This surprised him. He eyed her. "About what?"

"I haven't been honest with you."

"Oh?"

"My opinions," she said, her sneakers padding over the soft ground. "Do you realize the whole time we were together I never let myself get angry with you?"

Gus had never thought about that. "If you're fixing for a fight..." He stepped off the path, out of the way of other walkers, then dropped his arms to his sides. "Go ahead, let me have it."

"Not that kind of fight. But I am hopping mad." Her eyes flashed in definite battle mode. "I don't understand you, Gus. How could you walk away from me and what we had together?"

In full agreement, he pulled at the bill of his baseball cap. "That's what—"

She jabbed her finger in his chest. "You do not get to interrupt me. I'm speaking my truth, and you need to listen."

This feisty side of her was new—and hot. Intrigued, he nodded.

"I love you, Gus, and I think if you gave us half a chance, you'd come to see that you love me, too. There, I said it." Hands on her hips, she nodded for him to speak.

"I'm with you. We belong together."

Her anger seemed to fade away. "It's about time you figured that out."

Eager to reach his destination a few yards away, he grasped her hand and pulled her forward, cutting between trees and plants, until he reached the lofty ash where lovers came to seal their futures. "It's this thick skull of mine. I always said we made quite a pair, but I didn't realize... The thing is..."

His throat was so tight, he had trouble swallowing, let alone getting the words out.

They needed to be said, and this was the right place to do it. He removed his shades, then hers, and dropped them carefully to the ground. "I love you, Wanda. I think I have since the day we worked on the Lincoln together."

Warmth lit her eyes. "That's around the same time I started to fall for you. I fought my feelings because I didn't trust you. No, wait. I didn't trust that the real me was enough for anyone to love."

"I'm crazy about the real you."

"You don't really know me. I've been hiding my opinions and what I really want. I'm through holding back. If something bothers me, you'd better believe you'll hear about it. I expect we'll have some arguments. The thought terrifies me, but I have to be myself. Can you deal with that?"

"I like this spunky side of you." He smiled into her eyes. "All I've ever asked was for you to be yourself."

"You mean that?"

He nodded. "I wouldn't want to fight day and night, but it's bound to happen from time to time. That's okay as long as we make up after."

"I hear that can be fun."

"You've been straight with me, now it's my turn," he said. "Making a commitment has always scared me crapless. This is going to sound nuts, but my issues came from when my mother left, way back when."

"That doesn't sound crazy to me. I'm not sure what you're getting at, though." She squinted. "You're going to have to spell it out."

"Why do you think we're standing under this particular ash tree?"

"This is the one people talk about?" She glanced

around in wonder, then shook her head at him. "I thought you didn't believe in any of those stories about that 'old myth.'"

"Changed my mind." He grasped both her hands in his. "I love you, Wanda, and I'm committed to this relationship, regardless what comes up. Are you on board?"

She nodded, tugged him down and kissed him.

Holding her felt right. *Home.* He rested his forehead against hers. "Is that a yes?"

"The kind that means forever."

He kissed her again, several times before she squirmed out of his grasp. "As much as I like this, it's sweltering out here."

Gus had to agree. He also wanted to be alone with her. "Let's go to your place. I'll give you a ride to your car, and we'll meet there."

As soon as they stepped into her apartment, he grinned. "I could use a shower."

"You and me both."

Sometime later, after steamy shower sex, he sprawled beside Wanda in bed. "If you're free tonight, I'd like to take you to dinner at Ellen's."

Propped on her arm, she frowned. "Why Ellen's? To use your own words, the restaurant is stuffy and frou-frou."

"Yeah, but you said you've always wanted to go."

"You remember that?"

"I remember everything you say."

"What about your standing dinner with Polly and your dad?"

"I cancelled."

"Was Polly unhappy about the change in plans?"

"Actually, she was pretty cool. I didn't explain anything, but she guessed. She wished me good luck. Did she tell you she's moving into Sunny Horizons next weekend?"

Wanda nodded. "What a relief, huh? She's going to be happy about us. It's probably too late to get a reservation at Ellen's."

"On the off-chance you'd say yes, I called earlier and got us a table."

"You certainly are cocky."

He kissed the crook of her shoulder. "No, I'm determined to make you happy."

AFTER AN AMAZING MEAL at Ellen's, Wanda let out a contented sigh. "The food here is excellent. And this triple layer chocolate cake? Heaven on a plate. Thanks for bringing me here, Gus."

His eyes lit with love. "My pleasure."

He really loved her—the real her. Wanda basked in the knowledge and trusted he would for a long time.

"What are you smiling about?" he said, snagging a forkful of her dessert.

"I don't think I've ever felt this amazing. About myself and us—even if you did steal some of my cake."

"Hey, you closed your eyes and moaned over your first bite. What choice did I have?" he teased. Then he grew serious. "Have I mentioned I love you?"

"About a dozen times, but I wouldn't mind hearing it again."

He took her hand. "I love you, Wanda."

"Aww, I love you, too. Now give me back my fork."

He chuckled. "Yes, ma'am."

"Will you let me help with Polly's move?"

"You bet. Did she tell you I bought the house?"

Wanda nodded. "That's so great."

"For both Aunt Polly and me. I'll be doing some renovations. I'd like your input."

"Okay. What do you have in mind?"

"For starters, updating the kitchen and baths."

"I'll pick up a few home decorating magazines, but I doubt I'll be much help. I think you should hire someone who knows what they're doing."

"I will, but your opinions are important to me."

"Because?"

"Down the road, I picture you moving in, and us raising a couple kids there."

Wanda could hardly believe her ears. "Are you saying what I think you are?"

"Yep. You and me—marriage."

She laughed. "What did you do with the real Gus Viggio?"

"He smartened up. I want the whole nine yards. You by my side forever and a bunch of little Gusses and Wandas keeping us on our toes."

Six weeks ago, she'd have killed for a proposal and the promise of her dreams coming true. With her new-found confidence, she was in no hurry. "We're just getting back together. It's too soon to talk marriage."

"That used to be my line. Will you at least give me a chance?"

"Let's give each other a chance."

"Thank you." His eyes suspiciously damp, Gus lifted his wine glass. "To the woman of my dreams and the love of my life."

Wanda also teared up. "I love you, too, so much. Ask me again, later."

"I will."

"We should call Polly, Cindy and your sister, and

tell them we're back together."

"They can wait. I'd rather go to your place and show you how much I love you."

And he did.

THE END

THANK you for letting me share my stories with you!

There are 12 sexy firefighter books planned for the **Heroes of Rogue Valley: Calendar Guys**

IF YOU ENJOYED **MR. MARCH**, help others find this book by recommending it to your friends and by writing a review. If you would like to know when my next release is available and other fun stuff, sign up for my newsletter here: www.annroth.net

VISIT ME AT FACEBOOK FACEBOOK.COM/ANN-ROTHAUTHORPAGE

Follow me on Twitter @Ann_Roth

Email me at ann@annroth.net

Visit my website www.annroth.net

THANKS, and until next time,

Ann

PLEASE ENJOY this excerpt from **Mr. January:**

SENIOR FIREFIGHTER ADAM HEALEY is a man with a mission: get promoted to lieutenant at the Guff's Lake Fire Department. It's time, but more important, the promotion will finally earn him the respect of his dying father. Single mom Samantha Everett's deadbeat ex has left her to fend for herself, and she's working hard to support her young son with her baking business. Neither Adam nor Samantha is looking for a relationship. But love has a way of surprising people...

AT THE UNGODLY hour of five-forty-five a.m., Samantha Everett pulled into the delivery slot at Rosemary's Breakfast Nook. In the dark, the twin beams of the hatchback's headlights spotlighted the swirling snow. Well, it was early January in Rogue Valley.

"Please don't stick," she muttered under her breath, dreading the thought of putting on the tire chains.

Although so far, she hadn't needed them. When she'd moved to Guff's Lake six months earlier, locals had assured her that the usual winter temperatures tended to hover above freezing.

So different from the bone-chilling cold and frequent snowstorms in Enterprise.

"Look, Mom! Snow!" William chimed from the backseat.

At the age of five, he was delighted by almost everything—even at this hour. His joy was contagious, and Samantha's irritation dissipated like smoke. "I see it."

"Let me out." He unbuckled his car seat straps and bounced in anticipation for her to open the door.

Yawning—thanks to only five hours' sleep— Samantha exited the car. The building's perimeter lights cast long shadows across the nearly vacant concrete lot, a large area shared by several businesses. The few cars here now belonged to Rosemary, the cook, and wait staff. Rosemary's Breakfast Nook served the best breakfast in town, and snow or none, when the café opened at six, business would be brisk.

Despite the relative stillness, it was best to be safe. "Hold onto my coat," she directed.

Her itching-to-be-independent son grumbled but obeyed. Samantha opened the hatchback and jockeyed a dolly cart to the pavement. William helped her unfold it. Then she carefully loaded it with today's order—eight dozen still-warm cinnamon rolls, and six dozen each assorted muffins and scones. Her biggest order to date would net her more money than she'd ever earned as a baker in Enterprise.

Rosemary wouldn't pay her until a week from Friday, but Samantha had already divided and earmarked every penny. Groceries and other household expenses, bakery supplies, and the savings account for attorney fees.

To date, Jeff had ignored every one of the financial and custodial obligations spelled out in the divorce decree. Not one penny of child support or money for the debts he'd saddled her with, and not one request to see his son. Good riddance!

After all this time, Samantha doubted she'd ever hear from Jeff. She didn't need an attorney right now, but Betty Randall, her grandmotherly neighbor, believed that she did. Just in case. The woman had been so insistent Samantha had lost sleep over it. Mainly because Betty gave sound advice, unlike the unsolicited guidance from Samantha's parents.

William helped push the dolly toward the delivery entrance. As always, the door was unlocked for her, and easy to shoulder open and back through. Pausing inside the door, she brushed the snow off her son's parka and hat and then took care of her own coat.

The warmth, the fragrant aroma of freshly brewing coffee, and the haze from the sizzling vat of oil greeted her. A fragrant, smoky scent filled the air, and Samantha's mouth watered.

"Good morning," she greeted Rosemary and her longtime boyfriend and cook, José.

Round and perpetually cheerful, the forty-something restaurant owner greeted Samantha and William with her usual toothy smile. "Good morning." She winked at William. "How are you, sunshine?"

His small brow furrowed. "My name is William Tyler Everett Jones." Samantha had changed her last name back to Everett but had left her son's name intact.

From the time he'd first formed sentences, he'd insisted that everyone use his given name.

"I know that, darlin', but seeing you always makes me smile, and a true smile is as warm as the sunshine," Rosemary said. "Do you two have time for breakfast this morning?"

"Say yes, Mom." William gave Samantha the round-eyed, pleading look she'd never been able to resist.

Guff's Lake Bed & Breakfast, her only other paying client so far, didn't expect her until seven, and William's half-day kindergarten wouldn't start for several hours yet. She ought to use the time on housework—keeping the kitchen spotless was a constant chore.

But she really could use another cup of coffee and something to eat besides the bowl of cold cereal waiting for her at home.

"We'd love to have breakfast here," she said. "Can I put in an order for José's hash browns?"

José chuckled. "You bet. Bacon and eggs, too?"

"Yes, please."

"And cocoa?" William asked, going all round-eyed again.

Rosemary nodded. "I'll bring it with your breakfast."

As she filled a coffee mug for Samantha, Jana, one of the waitresses and Samantha's best friend, entered the kitchen through the restaurant's swinging doors.

"I thought I heard you in here. Can you believe it's snowing? I'll bet you love that, William. Let's get the case loaded."

Samantha wheeled the dolly to the counter out front, where bright walls and colorful posters added a homey, cheerful feel to the restaurant. She and William kept Jana company while she arranged Samantha's baked goods in the case and placed the printed "Treats by Samantha" sign in plain view. What didn't fit stayed in the delivery boxes for restocking the case until the restaurant closed at one.

Rosemary inspected the finished display with a satisfied nod. "You and William go on and make yourselves at home," she told Samantha. "I'll bring your food out shortly."

Samantha let her son choose where to sit. He led her to his favorite spot, a booth in front of the big picture window that faced the door. With the restaurant minutes from opening, Jana and the three other servers bustled around, seeing to last-minute details. Then one of the waitresses unlocked the door and welcomed in the morning's first customers.

Moments later, Rosemary delivered breakfast to Samantha and William. While Samantha enjoyed her food and coffee, her son chattered nonstop. During recess at Guff's Lake Elementary, the school he proudly called his own, he would have a snowball fight and build a snowman with Douglas and Harper, his two best friends.

Customers steadily streamed in to eat at the restaurant or collect their breakfast and morning coffee to go, some alone, others in groups. The almost twenty thousand Guff's Lake residents tended to be a friendly bunch, and even the people Samantha didn't recognize greeted her with nods and smiles.

Sipping a second cup of coffee and staring out the window with relief as the snow let up, she watched an orange 4Runner pull into the lot. A solid-looking male slid out of the driver's seat. Dressed in a leather bomber jacket, jeans, and a baseball cap, he wore a cast on one foot and a sling on his arm. A backpack swung from the other shoulder. Even with his arm injury and hobbling gait, he managed to move with a purposeful stride that for some reason reminded her of a big, sleek jungle cat. A tiger or a puma came to mind.

The sky had lightened a fraction, and between the approaching dawn and the perimeter lights, she easily made out his face.

And oh, what a face! The broad forehead, strong chin, and straight nose only added to his overall attractiveness. With a jolt of awareness, she recognized him. Adam Healey, aka Mr. January in the Guff's Lake Fire Department calendar that had come out last month, just in time for Christmas, as part of an ongoing fund-raising drive for the fire department's benefit fund.

The calendar featured twelve of the most gorgeous men Samantha had ever laid eyes on, and listed fascinating information, including height, weight, and marital status. She recalled that Adam was single.

Every female in town, along with a host of men and all the local businesses, had purchased calendars. At Rosemary's Breakfast Nook, the calendar hung prominently in the display case, with Adam in his firefighter hat, grinning and shirtless under a deep blue sky. In the background, the snowy Siskiyou Mountains. Samantha glanced at it and blew out an admiring sigh.

Everyone knew that the guys from the Guff's Lake Fire Department hung out here, since the station a was mere two blocks away. Ordinarily Samantha came and went before any of them wandered in for coffee and breakfast. But today…

Adam must have sensed her staring at him, for his gaze met hers through the window. Embarrassed, she turned her attention to William.

"—read more *Charlotte's Web* to us today," he said, still chattering about his kindergarten class.

"That's such a great book," she replied.

The door opened, and a gust of cold air rushed in. But the man who shut it behind him sucked the chill right out of the room.

Adam's eyes were still riveted on her. She couldn't seem to tear her glance away, either. Up this close, his pale-blue eyes were even more striking than they were in the calendar photo. The color of the sky just before the sun rose.

It had been a while since a man turned her head, and she wasn't sure she liked that fluttery feeling of attraction. She'd moved here to escape Enterprise and the past and start fresh, and for the first time in more than three years, she was happy. Between taking care of William and supporting the two of them with her baked-goods business, socializing with friends and a weekly knitting class, she had filled her life to the brim. She didn't have time to look at a man, let alone date.

Or so she assured herself.

Ready to leave, she pushed to her feet and stacked her breakfast dishes to make cleanup easier for Jana. Her friend sashayed toward Adam with her hips swaying and a longing look on her face.

Jana was dating someone, but she wasn't blind. By the similar expressions the other waitresses wore, they were just as smitten. So were the other women in the café, who checked Adam out with approval.

"Hey there, Adam," Jana said with a flirty smile. "I didn't expect to see you this early in the morning. How are that wrist and ankle?"

"Getting better every day."

"Adam!" Rosemary bustled over with a grin on her face. "You're just in time to meet Samantha Everett, the bakery goddess behind Samantha's Treats, the goodies that bring you back every morning. Adam's a huge fan," she told Samantha.

"That's right. Hey." He touched the bill of his hat.

He was a big man, a good six inches taller than Samantha and powerfully built. Even wearing ankle boots that added two inches to her five-feet-six-inch height, she felt small.

"Hi," she answered, cupping her empty mug to her chest. As if it could deflect the mesmerizing warmth in his eyes.

"William, this is Adam Healey," Rosemary continued. "He's a firefighter."

"For real?" Her son looked starstruck.

"How you doing, sport?" Adam asked.

"My name is William Tyler Everett Jones."

"That's quite a mouthful. Mind if I call you sport?"

"Okay."

This was a first, and surprised Samantha.

Adam sniffed. "I smell smoke."

Right then, a waitress hurried out of the kitchen balancing several plates. Wisps of smoke followed her. The smoke alarm screeched, and people stopped eating.

"Everyone, clear out," Adam ordered in a booming voice. "Keep an eye on this." He handed his backpack to Samantha. On his way to the kitchen he pulled his arm from the sling, whipped out his phone and made a call.

"What's that noise? Where is he going, Mom?" William asked as he and Samantha donned their coats and headed toward the door.

"To see what set off the smoke detector."

"Why can't we go with him?"

"We don't want to get in the way. Besides, we need to get going." But she had Adam's backpack and she'd left her dolly behind the display case.

She would have handed the backpack to someone and come back later for the dolly, but her son dug in his heels. "I want to wait and see what happens," he said, his breath clouding in the cold.

The stubborn set of his jaw reminded her of Jeff when they were still married. Before he'd walked away from her and William, just days before her twenty-seventh birthday. The last time William had seen his father, he'd been all of twenty-six months old. Yet somehow, he'd picked up that stubborn look.

Getting him into the car without a battle wouldn't be easy, and Samantha didn't have the energy for an argument. With a sigh, she nodded and waited out front with the other restaurant patrons.

~

A BURNER HAD CAUGHT FIRE, and thick smoke rapidly filled the kitchen. Adam grabbed the fire extinguisher and went to work. In seconds, he had the flames out.

"Open the back door and get some fresh air in here," he directed.

Rosemary complied, and José swiped his brow. "That was close. I shouldn't have set that towel so close to the flames. It won't happen again."

Adam nodded. "Hang on while I call the station." He made the call then disconnected. "They're coming anyway. It's what we do."

His sprained wrist hurt like hell. Should've been more careful when he'd hefted the extinguisher. But his focus had been on putting out the fire before something really bad happened, and he'd forgotten to think about himself.

He started to massage it, winced, and slipped it back into the sling. With any luck, it would continue to mend, and he could start light duty next week. Eight hours a day, five days a week, doing filing and other administrative work. Not his job of choice. He preferred working a pair of back-to-back, twenty-four-hour shifts, fighting fires, or serving as a paramedic. Still, light duty beat sitting at home, twiddling his thumbs, and trying to study. The two weeks he'd just suffered through was more than enough time off.

"When did you last have a fire and life safety training refresher?" he asked Rosemary.

"I'm not sure. Maybe a year? Do you remember, José?"

"I'd say more like two."

This year, Nate was in charge of safety training, and

Adam made a mental note to let him know to schedule something here. For all he knew, Nate might be on the engine today. Since Adam had been forced to take disability leave, he'd lost track of who did what this month.

"Let's clean up this mess and get back to work," Rosemary said.

José nodded. "I'll toss everything I was cooking, and start over."

"I'll let our customers know," Rosemary said. "Adam, how about coffee and a treat on the house?"

He couldn't argue with that. "A scone and an espresso sound good. Make it a double. I need the extra caffeine. This studying is a real bear."

Rosemary frowned. "What are you studying for?"

"The exam I need to pass so I can get promoted to lieutenant." That was the next rung up from senior firefighter and one rank below captain. Adam already knew a lot of what he needed for the job, but the class he'd enrolled in focused on management skills, which he didn't have. He'd made it more than halfway through the sixteen-week course, but there was still a lot to learn before the written test in late February. The class and the studying were rougher than he'd expected.

He returned to the restaurant and watched the diners file inside again.

In the midst of that, Rafe, Daniel, Hank, and Max strode in, just as Adam had known they would. Big men, decked out in fire gear.

"Like I told you, it's been handled," Adam greeted them.

"You know the drill," Adam's best bud, Rafe, replied.

Adam's crewmates tromped into the kitchen to

make sure the fire was out and check for fire within the walls.

Samantha and her kid returned to their booth. She handed him his backpack.

"Mind if join you?" Adam asked.

When the little guy grinned, she shrugged. "Okay.

Adam slid in beside him, putting him across from Samantha. He'd heard about her—divorced, moved to Guff's Lake six months ago, house-sitting Lucy Marks's place while the older woman wintered in Palm Desert.

She was a looker—short black hair, long, wispy bangs, big eyes, and a sexy mouth that made him think of pleasure. But he didn't get involved with single mothers. He never had, mainly because most of them were looking for husbands. And judging by the relationships Adam had screwed up, he figured he'd make a lousy husband and father.

"Was it a big fire?" the boy asked. He had his mother's eyes.

"It could have been," Adam said. "But it's all good now."

William nodded somberly. "What happened to your arm and leg?"

Adam shrugged. "I hurt them fighting a fire." With his wrist still screaming, he figured he'd set himself back. That really teed him off, and not only because he wanted back on regular duty. Until he healed, he couldn't take the physical exam he needed to qualify for lieutenant.

Between the management class, the written and physical exams, and the interview, the whole process would take roughly four months. Time he couldn't afford to make up later, not if he wanted his father to see him promoted.

To finally make him proud. Adam wanted that just about more than he'd ever wanted anything.

His buds returned to the restaurant, stopping at the booth where Adam sat.

Every one of them looked Samantha over.

"Hello. I'm Rafe Donato." Flashing the twin dimples that had women falling all over him, Rafe shook her hand.

"This is Samantha and her son, William," Adam said by way of introduction. "I just met them myself. Samantha makes all that stuff in the front case."

"So you're the talent behind those scones. I'm Max Meier."

Max also shook her hand. Women said his brown eyes were soulful, and Samantha looked as if she bought that hook, line, and sinker.

Adam didn't like it, but what did he care? "These two other guys are Daniel and Hank."

Lanky Daniel grinned, and Hank, the station's newest and most solemn firefighter, nodded.

Each of them shook hands with her kid, who was all eyes.

Other diners came over to say hello. Adam didn't miss the looks women gave him and his buds. They were used to that.

A moment later, Rafe checked his watch. "We're a little over an hour until the end of our second shift. We should go."

The crew's back-to-back shifts started at eight a.m. on Mondays and ended at eight a.m. on Wednesdays, when another crew took over.

"Good to meet you, William. Samantha." Rafe nodded to Rosemary and the waitresses. "I'll see you ladies for breakfast shortly."

As they filed out, Adam swore he heard collective female sighs.

Although Samantha seemed immune to his crew-mates' charms. Adam wasn't about to examine why he felt relieved.

"We should leave now, too," Samantha said. "We still have another delivery to make, and then William needs to get ready for school."

Already standing, the boy cupped his groin and danced from foot to foot. "Mom, I gotta pee."

Samantha gave Adam a Kids, what can you do? look and then slid quickly from the booth. "Hurry, before you have an accident."

"I don't wanna use the girls' bathroom."

"Well, I can't go into the men's."

"I'll take him," Adam offered.

Unsure whether she should trust this man she'd just met with her son, Samantha hesitated. "That isn't necessary."

"I gotta go right now," William insisted.

"He's a good guy," Janna added from a nearby table, where she was pouring coffee.

Samantha relaxed. Anyway, there was no time to argue. Adam ferried her son toward the men's room. "Sit tight, Sam," he said over his shoulder. "We'll be right back."

~

SAM. Adam had called her Sam. Samantha sat back in the booth and sighed. She didn't go by the shortened version of her name anymore, hadn't since high school. Even her parents called her Samantha.

She kind of liked hearing it again on Adam's lips.

Not that she was interested in him. She wasn't, she assured herself.

By the time he brought her son back, she was up and waiting with her coat on and holding out William's.

"Thanks, Adam." She helped her son into his parka.

"No prob. Be good, sport."

"I will."

"Hey, I'll be back at work next week. If you ever want to visit the fire station, give me a call and I'll show you two around." Adam wrote his cell number on the back of his card.

"Really?" William looked as if it was Christmas morning.

Samantha preferred to steer clear of the firefighter she was attracted to, but she couldn't bear to disappoint her son. "We just might take you up on that."

A tour to please William, and that would be that. As they headed toward the car, she pushed the firefighter from her thoughts.

PLEASE ENJOY this excerpt from **Mr. February**:

RAFE DONATO IS a senior firefighter well aware that loving a woman can destroy a man. He will never trust any female with his heart. Jillian Metzger is a talented potter whose biological clock is ticking. Ready to fall in love, get married and start a family, Jillian wants what Rafe cannot give.

. . .

"Come back here, Pooh!" Jillian Metzger shouted as she sprinted across the uneven field adjacent to the cottage.

The Border collie had the gall to bark joyfully and skip over rocks and tree roots at a clip Jillian couldn't begin to keep up with.

To make matters worse, it started to rain. She hadn't taken the time to grab an umbrella, let alone a jacket—she'd simply darted out of the studio in hot pursuit. Not wise, considering temperatures in early March in Rogue Valley tended to be on the south side of chilly.

If and when she managed to catch Pooh, she was going to let her freeloading brother have it. Why couldn't JR keep an eye on his own dog? Because he'd gone out with Chelsea, frittering his day away when he should have been looking for a job.

Pooh was a good fifty yards ahead now, and Jillian quickly losing steam. She was on the verge of collapsing in exhaustion when the dog finally skidded to a stop. Tail wagging, Pooh changed course, trotting toward a man and woman standing slightly uphill, under a big umbrella. What were they doing here in the boonies on a rainy Wednesday morning?

Jillian lurched to a halt to catch her breath and pull herself together before they noticed her. A futile effort, given that she was a sodden mess. Leaning against the trunk of a lofty tree heavy with leaf buds, she tucked her dripping hair behind her ears with icy fingers.

She couldn't tear her gaze from them. What a striking couple. The dark-haired male, muscled and at least six feet tall, wore jeans, a light-blue sports shirt, and a black windbreaker that hugged his broad shoulders. His companion, with her shiny, stylish haircut and designer suit, stood close beside him under the umbrella.

Something about the guy seemed vaguely familiar, but before Jillian could place him, Pooh did the unthinkable—raced forward, jumped up, and planted her muddy paws on his powerful thigh.

"Get down, Pooh!" Jillian cried, pushing away from the trees and running again.

The big man didn't seem all that upset. He patted the dog and then brushed the mud off his jeans, which were neatly pressed, as was his shirt. Clutching the umbrella in both hands, his horrified companion quickly stepped out of reach.

The second his dark gaze met Jillian's, she recognized him. What red-blooded woman could forget those mesmerizing eyes, the strong jaw, and the slight hollows of his cheeks? She was about to come face-to-face with Rafe Donato, aka Mr. February in the Guff's Lake Fire Department calendar.

The calendar, part of the ongoing fund-raising drive for the department's benefit fund, had been released right before Christmas and featured twelve of the most gorgeous firefighters...

Drop-dead, movie-star-handsome Rafe looked even better in person than his photo—if that was even possible. Jillian's heart lifted in an appreciative sigh.

The calendar included certain important facts about each firefighter, stats any woman with a pulse would want to know. According to the details Jillian recalled—and with a calendar hanging on the wall in her studio, she was quite familiar with them—Rafe was single. At least he had been when the calendar was printed. By the intimate look from his lady friend, his status had changed.

"I'm sorry about Pooh," she apologized. "She's supposed to stay in the yard. Instead, the little scamp dug under the fence and lit out."

When Pooh had made her escape, Jillian had been in her pottery studio, creating pieces for one of her retail customers and for the Rogue Valley Arts Festival. If she hadn't decided to stretch her back and wander to the window, she wouldn't have noticed until the dog was long gone.

"My dog used to do the same thing."

Rafe flashed a smile, revealing dimples—holy cow, dimples—and extended his arm.

"Rafe Donato."

Wishing she'd dressed in something other than raggedy work clothes, Jillian wiped her palms on her threadbare, damp jeans before she shook his huge hand. His firm, warm grip engulfed her cold fingers, and his chocolate-brown eyes fixed intently on her.

Her knees wobbled. She glanced away. As attractive as Rafe was, she refused to go all weak and fluttery. He was already taken.

Even if he hadn't been, the ramrod straight posture, military-short hair, meticulously pressed shirt and jeans, and polished black boots screamed order and control. This was the kind of man who made life miserable for everyone around him. At eighteen, she'd left home to get away from that. She would never go back.

Pooh licked Jillian's hand. "Bad girl," she said, but the dog's innocent expression was hard to resist.

Rafe's girlfriend cleared her throat. "I'm Sonia Kaye, Rafe's architect." She started to extend her hand, but, after giving Jillian a quick once-over, offered her card and a perfunctory smile instead. "I should go, Rafe. I've seen enough for now, and I took plenty of photos. I'll be in touch."

"Let me walk you to your car." He held up a finger, signaling Jillian to wait.

Pooh wanted to follow the couple, but Jillian caught hold of her collar. "You're not going anywhere." The dog put wet-dog smell on a whole new level, and Jillian grimaced. "You need a bath."

With JR and Chelsea out, who knew where—they certainly hadn't said good-bye or left a note, but then, they never did—she would likely be the one doing the honors.

Rafe and his architect girlfriend moved in tandem up a gently sloping hill, toward the two expensive sedans parked on a dirt patch some distance away—one, a silver Mercedes, the other a gleaming navy convertible BMW.

Which belonged to him? The sleek BMW, Jillian guessed. It looked cleaner and somehow suited him.

Yep, the convertible was his. Rafe held the umbrella over Sonia's head while she climbed into a silver Mercedes. After flashing a flirty smile, she drove away, her tires churning up mud.

Rafe tromped back to Jillian. "Where do you and Pooh live?"

"Not far. On the other side of the field."

He nodded. "Cy Jackson's property."

"How do you know the name of my landlord?"

"I just bought the two-acre plot you're standing on, and I know everything about this area. Your cottage isn't more than a third of a mile from here, an easy walk, but this driving rain can make even a short distance seem like a long way. How about a lift?"

The offer surprised her. "We couldn't possibly. We're both wet and muddy, and Pooh stinks something terrible." She held her nose.

Rafe didn't argue with her. "You don't even have an

umbrella. I do. I also happen to have a spare leash in the trunk of my car. Let me grab it, and I'll walk you and Pooh home."

~

JILLIAN WAS TALL, the top of her head almost level with Rafe's nose. That put her at about five-foot-ten. Long-limbed and slender, she could pass for a runway model—at least from what Rafe imagined. In baggy, wet clothes and dirty sneakers, he couldn't tell.

Her wet, shoulder-length blonde hair lay plastered to her head. Rafe remembered how cold her hand had felt in his. Any minute, her teeth would start to chatter.

"Here," he said, setting the umbrella down to shrug out of his lined windbreaker. "Put this on."

"But I'm a dirty mess."

"You're also freezing cold." He helped her into it then picked up the umbrella and held it over them. "Don't worry, it's washable. Zip up."

She did. The thing swam on her, which was kind of cute.

"How long have you lived on Cy's property?" he asked.

"For almost a year. Last month, I signed a lease for another year."

"We'll be neighbors, then—once I get my house built."

When not at the Guff's Lake Fire Department, Rafe spent his time managing his rental properties. He also kept an eye out for fixer-uppers, which he enjoyed re-modeling and selling. With the combined income he earned, he'd finally saved enough to build his dream home without emptying his bank account.

"Your own custom place? Lucky you. Sonia must be so excited."

"Because I hired her to design the house?"

"That and because you're a couple."

He laughed. "We're not together."

"Oh." Jillian looked surprised. "I assumed... You know."

"Getting romantically involved with my architect could be risky."

"Because if it didn't work out, you'd still need her help."

That and because as much as he liked women, and he liked them a lot, he didn't trust a single one enough to live with. Which wasn't quite true—he trusted his paternal grandma and a handful of female teachers from grade school and high school. But he preferred living alone. "Yeah."

Jillian nodded then angled her head. "You're a firefighter, right?"

"You've seen the calendar."

She blushed, adding much-needed color to her pale skin. "I have."

She had a generous mouth and fine, delicate features. "There's something on your chin," he noted, nodding at the gray glob stuck on the underside. The same stuff stained the cuff of her oversize sweatshirt. "And on your sleeve."

She touched the spot on her chin and rubbed at it, laughing self-consciously. "It's clay. I'm a potter."

"Ah. You do that full-time?"

"Yes. I sell to a couple of stores in the area an online. I'm also working on pieces for the Rogue Valley Arts Festival in Medford next month. Until recently, I also taught at the Artist Cooperative on the south side of town."

"You don't teach there anymore?"

"The school closed up shop last month. I'm getting ready to offer classes in my home studio."

"I never figured that little house with room for a studio."

"Actually, I use the outbuilding behind the cottage. With heat, electricity, and a skylight, it's perfect. I think it was originally designed as a workshop for household projects. I got permission from Cy to turn it into my pottery studio. My kiln is behind the building."

Rafe wondered how she made ends meet selling pottery and teaching classes. Having spent the first ten years of his life with his mom, whose sales from herbal concoctions and tie-dye T-shirts had often left them both hungry and moving in a hurry to escape eviction for non-payment of rent, he preferred a steady job with a regular paycheck, and money in the bank.

As they neared the cottage, Pooh woofed and strained at her leash.

"*Now* you want to get home," Jillian quipped. Under her breath, she added, "You'll change your tune when you realize you're about to get a bath."

Rafe chuckled, caught himself, and frowned. He wouldn't let this woman charm him.

Tibetan prayer flags were strung across the eaves over the porch. That and the aging VW van parked behind the hatchback in the gravel driveway reminded him of the years he'd lived with his mom.

Jillian frowned. "It's about time JR got back."

Rafe figured JR was her boyfriend. He wasn't about to ask—didn't want to know, but the words slipped out. "Who's JR?"

"My brother," she grumbled. "Thanks for walking me home, and for loaning me your jacket."

His unwitting gaze dropped to her plump, inviting lips. Jerking his attention to the jacket, he held out his hand for it.

"Let me clean it first. I'm happy to drop it off at the fire station later."

The guys were sure to razz him. He shrugged. "Sure. I won't be in again until Monday."

"Then you're a part-time firefighter?"

He shook his head. "I work Mondays and Tuesdays, two back-to-back, twenty-four-hour shifts. That's forty-eight hours a week, with five days off in between."

"Your days off sound nice, but isn't it dangerous, working such long hours with no break?"

"We each have a place to bunk at night, so I usually get some sleep. Even on busy nights, I manage all right. After eleven years, I'd better." Ready to leave, he gestured at the cottage. "Stay dry."

He turned away and strode back toward his property.

ALSO BY ANN ROTH

Ann Roth Classics

A Place to Belong

Father of the Year

Another Life

My Sisters

Dunlin Shores

Book 1 Just the Way You Are

Book 2 Wedding Bell Blues

Book 3 Falling for Mr. Wrong

Book 4: A Special Kind of Love

Firefighters

Book 1 Mr. January

Book 2 Mr. February

Book 3 Mr. March

Book 4: Mr. April

Book 5: Mr. May

Book 6: Mr. June

Book 7: Mr. July

Book 8: Mr. August

Book 9: Mr. September

Book 10: Mr. December

Halo Island

Book 1 All I Want for Christmas

Book 2 The Pilot's Woman

Book 3 Ooh, Baby!

Book 4 The One I Love

Miracle Falls

Book 1 Christmas in Miracle Falls

Book 2 Dream a Little Dream

Book 3 It Had to Be You

Book 4: You're the One That I Want

Saddlers Prairie

Book 1 Since I Fell for You

Book 2 I'll Be There

Book 3 Until There Was You

ABOUT THE AUTHOR

Ann Roth is an award-winning author of 40-plus contemporary romance and women's fiction novels, as well as novellas and numerous short stories. Her first novel was published in 2000 by Harlequin Special Edition and was nominated by *Romantic Times* as best first book. Ann lives with the love of her life in the Greater Seattle area and enjoys creating flawed characters and putting them in challenging situations that help them grow and ultimately find love— whether or not they're looking for it.

Find out about new releases!
Sign up for my newsletter

Or visit my website www.annroth.net

www.ingramcontent.com/pod-product-compliance
Lightning Source LLC
Chambersburg PA
CBHW010540100726
47903CB00011B/3071